Blinding

A novel by
Marti Healy

© Copyright 2021, Marti Healy. All rights reserved.

Front and back cover photos, and page 5 author photo,
© Shelly Marshall Schmidt.

Pages 110-113, Jack the railroad tramp's stories were gleaned from
"Following the Tracks," © Dale Wickum.

Pages 176-177, "Mother Moon," is from Pueblo Indian Folk-Stories,
by Charles F. Lummis, New York: Century Co., 1910, public domain.

ISBN 978-0-9857018-7-1

Limited First Edition

Printed in U.S.A.

Published by The Design Group Press, LLC

The author would like to express her recognition and appreciation to
Barry Doss and Kim Noah for their dedication and talent brought to the
design and development of this book.

MARTI HEALY *Books*-
www.martihealybooks.com

This book is dedicated
with acknowledgement
and warm personal gratitude
to my friends:
singer Chad Mitchell, and
photographer/storyteller Dale Wickum.

Please visit YouTube or your favorite music service to listen to the music of Chad Mitchell and the Chad Mitchell Trio. You'll be particularly touched by the incredible renditions of "Dark as a Dungeon" and "She Was Too Good to Me" by Chad. They are breathtaking.

Please also visit the website: www.FollowingTheTracks.com by Dale Wickum for his amazing photographs and stories. His work is brilliant.

Behind the moon:

A message from the author.

I began writing professionally in the days of pencils and legal pads and typewriters. It was right about the time in which this book begins – the early 1970s.

Initially I wrote exclusively in the voices of others, as a copywriter for various radio stations, advertising agencies, and communications firms. I began writing in my own voice as a book author and freelance columnist in the early 2000s (I still start with a pencil in hand and a legal pad on my lap).

But "BLINDING THE MOON" has taken me to discovering entirely new voices in entirely new places with entirely new experiences.

This book is a work of fiction, and all characters and incidents are fiction. But I would not have been able to create it without the invaluable input, advice, material, and inspiration that were shared with me by two wonderful friends: Chad Mitchell, singer, and Dale Wickum, photographer/storyteller.

Although they have never even met each other, they do know how much of this book is actually drawn from their own life experiences, and how much was purely my imagination. I'm leaving it up to them to tell … or not … but I have undying gratitude to both of them for their contributions, trust, encouragement, and for allowing me to play fast and loose with the facts.

Both of them shared with me their life stories and reminiscences – about experiences and places in the world where I have never been, adventures and lifestyles for which I would never have had the courage, and encounters with people I would never have been privileged to know. And so, with their generous permission, I borrowed from these pieces of their lives.

I listened and leaned into their stories, and simply made up the rest. I imagined and empathized my way through all the senses and feelings and conversations. I researched and internalized and remembered the times and places.

In the telling of it all, I tried to bring to it my personal commitment to writing lyrically – to bring to the page the inherent rhythm and cadence and music of life. I particularly want the readers of my books to have an experiential sense of being there – to see and hear and smell and feel along with the characters. Sometimes with this particular book it was almost brutal. But, in the end, it brought me a sense of peace and understanding that I hope is passed along to the reader.

"BLINDING THE MOON" is a story that is rather picaresque in style, but not quite. A story that is real, but not quite. A story that is mine, but not quite. Perhaps it will become a story that rather belongs to you, the reader. And that will be fine.

PART ONE

The Arrest.

July 14th, 1972

There was a time when he was very young that he believed the moon to be omnipotent. He thought perhaps God lived in the moon, and perhaps that was the reason he was taught to say his prayers at night.

Most nights, he could see the moon through his bedroom window, and it watched over him. Until they moved – his mother and he moved – into the small apartment by themselves. And his side of the bed faced away from the window, and he could no longer see the moon with or without God living in it, and there was no one there that heard him praying, and so he felt as if he must be living on the wrong side of the moon, and it no longer cared to watch over him.

Perhaps if the moon had been watching him on that night all those years later, he would not have gone. But the clouds were thick, and they drew hot, dark blankets across the face of the sky. And the woman had not come, and he was alone with his secrets and crimes and decisions.

The rains had finally stopped a few hours earlier, but the clouds still hovered; they writhed and roiled as if competing for attention against the river rising below them. Yet still he decided to leave, to make the river crossing. And he wondered if part of the river's own churning discontent was because no one could even decide on its name – in Mexico, it's called the Rio Bravo and in Texas, it's the Rio Grande; but the river made no distinction for itself, nor did he as he was caught struggling in the middle of it, trying to swim across it.

He wasn't hard to find, even in the blackness of the night. He was flailing against the river's hidden current;

it was mucked with filth and debris, jutted with rocks, and he was completely naked and utterly vulnerable. The river wasn't particularly deep right there, but the slime of its bed made it impossible to get a foothold, while the unrelenting undertow kept dragging him farther south; it had already sucked off both his shoes, the only bit of clothing he had allowed himself to wear as he crossed it.

His capture had seemed sudden and surreal. He saw the lights first, blue and pulsing overhead – licking at the bottom of the sky; and then, thick white beams of light scraped across the surface of the brackish water surrounding him, giving everything the disconcerting look of an overexposed film negative, before blinding him with its intensity.

He was also startled by a sudden flash of accountability he felt amidst the absolute certainty of being caught, being arrested, being jailed. And swirling beneath it all, there seemed to be another sort of undertow, a suck of responsibility, perhaps of guilt, of anxiety about Suzanna. Suzanna and the dog.

Angry voices were shouting a mix of directions and profanity in two languages from both banks of the river, and the man tried to remember how to say, *don't shoot,* in both of them. But no one was shooting. And so he began lurching his way to the north bank, toward Texas and U.S. law enforcement. To the south were the "policìa" and Mexican jail – and the American justice system seemed to be the better option.

He began to understand why the woman had never come, even though he'd waited for her, out-waited the storms for her. He saw that the VW van was there, parked as a dark shadow outline on the U.S. bank of the river; but the woman's brother wasn't with it. He felt the urge welling up in him to call out their names, to shout out for them into the night, to curse and cry out to them both; but then he could hear the absurdity of it, and he found it rather interesting, compelling really, that he wasn't particularly angry or sorry for himself or even afraid.

    At the last possible moment, he thought to release the two backpacks that he was bringing across the river with him – his and the one the woman was supposed to have carried. They were filled with tightly bound, plastic-wrapped marijuana – as well as his clothing and wallet, his keys and credit cards, his watch and everything else of value. Thousands of dollars of the stuff would be flushed away in a matter of seconds. But without it, there would be no physical evidence to be found on him.

    The first backpack came away from his grasp easily, almost like a freed animal that had been thrashing against him the entire trip. It jumbled its way downriver and he watched it bob and sink and bob and sink. And he wondered if the searchlights would pick it up before it became lost to the current completely.   But he was struggling wildly with the second backpack: its straps and ties were water-sodden and refused to budge. He had fastened it over his shoulders and across his chest to free his arms for the crossing. But the river had swollen the woven material, and the buckles and knots would not release their grips. He pulled and tugged at it in growing desperation, trying to separate himself from its weight, the noose that encircled him, the culpability of its contents. But it was too late.

He came stumbling up out of the water and one of the waiting men reached out a hand to him and laughed, not unkindly, grabbing ahold of the backpack to pull him farther onto the shore.

They had to cut the pack off of him, literally sever the straps with knives, which left him shivering, thoroughly exposed and embarrassed; and so they gave him a blanket and he was grateful for its rough sense of protection, a sort of dark layer of dignity.

And all the while, he kept looking to the sky, trying to find the moon, trying to see if it could see him. He hoped it could not.

It was close to 2:00 a.m. and he was dressed in the dry clothing that had made it across the river with him – wrapped in plastic, shoved inside the backpack he couldn't release. But there had been no shoes in the pack, which confused and preoccupied him. He wondered if the shoes had been in the other backpack, or perhaps they had been taken by the law authorities who had stripped clean the pack they had cut off him. They'd gutted it as thoroughly as they had done the waiting van.

By this time, the single backpack had yielded its ten pounds of marijuana (along with the clothes he was now wearing, his wallet and identification, and the keys to the van). The van had been even more forthcoming, relieved of its interior panels, along with all its seats, carpet, roof lining, exterior wheels, tires, and hood. The forty-plus pounds of weed he and the girl and her brother had deposited there the night before the rains started had been revealed and recorded.

The man stood, looking at all the pieces and goods torn loose and left open, heaped and spread, examined and abandoned against the mud and muck and weeds. And again he thought of the woman and her brother and he flinched at his gullibility, his disposability. And it began to rain yet again.

He was seated in a plastic-encrusted booth at The Rose of Texas Café across from a Texas Ranger, the same one who had pulled him up from the river. The Ranger's name was Frank Flores and he was a Texan, born and bred. Flores drawled out his sentences with a peculiar pride found only in the Texan tongue, laced heavily with humor and sarcasm. The lawman had recognized the man even in his half-drowned state and through flashing lights in the dead of night.

"You really are that singer, that Kit Williams, aren't you?" Flores stated more than asked with a huge smile that wrapped around a fat, unlit cigar.

"Yes, Sir," Kit replied with as much courtesy and dignity as he could claim, still stinking of river, and looking down at the cheap plastic sandals on his feet that they had found for him to wear. They were flip-flops, extra large, bright pink. Kit winced at the color, and a voice in his head accosted him: *That's what you're focused on? The color of the stupid plastic shoes?*

A chipped and chromed jukebox in the corner of the café played Patsy Cline and Elvis Presley in alternating regularity. And then one of Kit's own songs came on and it filled him with embarrassment and Frank Flores chuckled softly. Kit held his tongue and refused to look away and smiled with a grace he couldn't possibly possess.

In a prophetic conversation months earlier, Kit's lawyer had advised him relative to being arrested: "Be polite, be cooperative, but tell them right away that you want a lawyer present before you answer any questions." Kit wondered at that possessive way he thought of Joel Menken: *his lawyer*. In actuality, Kit couldn't stand the man, didn't trust him. But Joel was just slick enough to let things slide and turn a deaf ear to something someone might need to tell him that was beyond strict legal boundaries. And smart enough to give pretty good advice. And disreputable enough to never have many clients and so was almost always available. Kit kept the lawyer's phone number memorized. He used to keep it in an address book, but that had apparently been in the other backpack and was somewhere south of Brownsville by then, so he was glad he had it in his head.

With or without legal counseling, Kit was being polite, he was being cooperative. He had been that way all of his life. Polite and cooperative. Polite to teachers, parents, people in authority, people not in authority, people who wanted things from him, people he wanted things from. And cooperative. Cooperative at school, cooperative with coaches, cooperative with bosses, cooperative with women, and priests, and librarians, and dogs, and grocery store checkout girls, and ticket-takers, and cab drivers, and drug dealers, and bartenders who wanted someone to come get his dad in the middle of the night or in the middle of the afternoon, and record producers, and business managers, and other musicians who were never going to see eye-to-eye with him. And policemen. He was always especially polite and cooperative with policemen. Somehow, policemen ranked right up there with his mother.

Everyone who knew Kit from his hometown of Fort Wayne, Indiana (pretty much everyone from the hometown of Fort Wayne, Indiana), could vouch for the politeness and cooperativeness of Kit Williams. From the time he started school, he was a local leader. He never consciously sought it out, but leadership seemed to seek and find him. He was president of every class through his senior year in high school – and then, he was president of the entire student body. He was even voted prom king.

      Kit was also captain of the high school track team. He discovered he could run – really run – when he was quite young. It was, in fact, the only time he had felt "true," somehow, like a whole, solid person. Even in the first grade, he was allowed to take himself to school, and he ran all the way. He was never quite sure if he was running to school or away from home – the too small, nondescript house where he lived as an only child with his parents, Ruth and Joe. Running the five blocks between his home and the school caused him to arrive early every morning, but that meant he could have the playground completely to himself for a short time. There was a small stand of trees at one end of the dirt-packed grounds where kids would play hide-and-seek and climb among the lower branches if there were no teachers nearby to forbid it. During his early-morning solitude, Kit would crouch low behind one of the larger trees and beat on it with his fists. But this often made his hands bleed, and caused concerned questions from his teacher and the school nurse, so he quickly turned to kicking the tree instead. He wore through his shoes faster that way, a fact that made him ashamed because he knew – was constantly being reminded – how expensive new shoes were. But he outgrew his single pair of shoes every year anyway, so he decided he could bear up under this particular guilt. What he couldn't bear up under was the constant rage between his parents. Then, sometime around the second or third grade, Kit began to separate himself from that world. It was like there became two Kits: one lived within the suffocating burden of adult anger and regret, the stench of drunkenness, and the ache of hearing his mother cry on the other side of the bathroom door; the other Kit had a perfectly normal childhood and home life, grew up to win trophies in track and field, was a natural leader, was a top student, was known as an especially nice boy, and was notably always polite and cooperative. One of the Kits also began in high school to occasionally steal cars.

Two weeks after Kit's ninth birthday, on Christmas Eve, 1945, Joe Williams didn't come home from work. Ruth calmly told her only son that his dad was in fact never coming home again. She had forbidden it. She never said as much, but Kit knew it was because of his dad's drinking. She also never said as much, but the boy sensed that he was expected to step up and become the man of the house. He spent a great deal of time over the following weeks, months, and years trying to figure out what that would entail, and what he had done to cause his dad to drink so much.

Barely into the first of the New Year, Kit found himself and his mother moving into a cramped, partially furnished apartment. It was a two-story walk up with one bedroom and one bed, a small bathroom that smelled of wet hair and mold and somebody else's urine, and a kitchen that barely held a Formica-topped table and two mismatched chairs next to a miniaturized chipped sink and a two-burner stove. An old-fashioned refrigerator was fitted into a sort of pantry-service porch around the corner from the kitchen itself; the appliance took up so much space that the alcove was virtually useless for any other purpose.

The apartment had been shoved into the back one-third of the upstairs of a leaning Victorian house in the older part of town. A larger apartment had been cobbled together in the front two-thirds of the floor and was rented by a distant relative of Kit's mother. Her name was Rene Sampson and she worked as a women's hairdresser and smelled constantly of permanent wave. Her own hairstyle would change from week-to-week; sometimes attractive to her perfectly round face, but at other times rather startling in overall appearance and color. Kit was never allowed to comment about it – to his mother or anyone else, he was cautioned. It wasn't the polite thing to do.

The landlady-owner of the house lived on the ground level. Her name was Mrs. Blackstone and that's what everybody called her (Kit assumed she had a first name, although he never heard it). Mrs. Blackstone's husband had been killed on the last day of the war; but the house had been converted into apartments long before that and, when Mr. Blackstone first went into the army, his wife naturally assumed the management of the building until he was to come home. Mrs. Blackstone always acted as if she expected him any day. She was a strongly built woman who never seemed to be a particular age. Her clothes never altered in style, nor did her hair color or her skin tone. She made wonderful potato salad and called Kit "the boy."

In the basement, among the clanging pipes and constant damp, a nearly blind "handyman" lived. Kit often felt sorry for the man, named Bruno (who, unlike Mrs. Blackstone, no one ever called by a last name). But Bruno had a thick German accent and Kit's mother said the man was lucky to find work at all, as well as a place to live, and Kit was not to bother him. Kit learned many years later that Bruno had lived there for the rest of his life and had lain dying in his bed for three days before anyone found him, a fact that bothered Kit far beyond what he could have explained.

The floors of the upper apartments, including the Williams', all slanted toward the center of the house where the common staircase climbed between the two stories. The whole upper floor seemed to sag under the weight of all the lives it had upheld over the decades, before and after its conversion to apartments: all the crying wet babies and soldiers home on leave, the siblings forced to share a room, the grandparents visiting one last time, the hopes and fears of new brides, the frustrations of old men, the teenagers packing for college and leaving home for new jobs in distant cities. And then it held the stoicism and humiliation of a 32-year-old divorced woman who had recently found employment as a personal secretary to a respected banker, and the acquiescent vulnerability of her nine-year-old boy.

☾

Kit spent what was left of the night he was arrested alone in a local sheriff's jail cell in the small river border town near where he had been captured. Texas Ranger Frank Flores had kept him at the café as long as he could. He'd bought him ham and eggs and pots of coffee, and they'd talked about Kit's professional experiences – from the early glory days with The Kit Williams Trio through his struggle to establish and maintain a solo career. Frank liked Kit a lot. He was a great fan of his music, his talent, his personality, his way of conducting himself under pressure. He hated to think about what now awaited the singer. Frank would carry an untidy assortment of guilt and justification about Kit's arrest for the rest of his life.

The local jail cell was overheated, the air overused. It smelled of ammonia and dirty water and leftover food. There was a sort of cot against one wall; small and hard, made out of rusty metal framing and a thin lumped mattress that had been heavily and frequently sprayed with a sickly sweet disinfectant to the point of permanently reeking of it. Better that than the alternative, Kit concluded as he hesitatingly stretched out on it. A soiled flat pillow and rough blanket were folded with unaccountable care at the foot of the cot. A toilet with no lid stood open to the room next to a small sink hung crookedly on the wall as the only other accommodations in the open-barred yet suffocating space. A misshapen roll of cheap toilet paper was balanced on the edge of the sink; looking damp and pitiful, it was grey and crinkled at the edges. Stacked roughly on the floor next to the sink was a pile of wafer-like tan paper towels, the kind that disintegrate into small brown patches when they touch wet skin and dry nothing.

In spite of everything, or perhaps because of everything, Kit slept for a couple of hours. He dreamed he was in his mother's bed again. The disinfectant smell was her perfume. She had rolled too close to him and he could feel her body heat overwhelming him. Her breath slid down his neck and back. He woke up suddenly, sweaty, with a miserable headache and an urgent need to relieve himself. But just then, they came and got him, and he realized that his cell floor – the entire Sheriff's office, in fact – was several inches deep in flood waters. And they told him that he and all the other prisoners in the surrounding areas were being transferred to higher ground; they'd found room for them all at the Huntsville State Penitentiary.

It was a rough, nauseating, six-hour ride to Huntsville in what must have been a decommissioned derelict school bus now outfitted with hard metal mesh over the windows and cages separating the driver and guards' seats from the prisoners. There were just five other prisoners in addition to Kit, plus two disinterested guards and a dispirited driver. Each prisoner was handcuffed to the back of the seat in front of him, but the chains were long enough that they were not particularly uncomfortable in their restraint. There were no shackles used on their ankles. Nobody spoke much to anyone else, with the exception of one dirt-dried old man who never ceased talking, mostly to himself, and mostly in Spanish; his clothes, hair, elephant-hide skin and beard stubble were almost the same faded color, all of it running together, grey and worn. The other prisoners slept most of the time, or at least pretended to. They all seemed to have been there before.

    Behind his own half-closed, sleep-deprived eyes, Kit rewound and replayed the scenes that were somehow predestined toward this untoward bus ride. They appeared to him in black and white and sepia tones. No color. With scratchy sounds. He couldn't quite catch some of the words. Perhaps they were mixed in with someone else's life. Or played out of order. For instance, he couldn't remember exactly why or even when he had turned his back on his music. The day he walked out on his promoter was clear enough. Jerry Fielding – Kit's professional manager, image builder, and confidant for more than a dozen years – had been oddly indifferent. Perhaps that's what made it so hard in the end. Or perhaps it was because this whole career path had become so hard. Nothing had come hard to Kit his entire life. This couldn't be right. It was much easier to get high.

  The drugs tended to be a blur, too. But effortless to acquire. It was the 1970s and he was a musician and he lived in New York City – The Village, in fact. It was wonderfully easy. At some point, the idea of importing and selling drugs for money became very attractive to him.

  Mercifully, a brief foray with cocaine ended fairly soon: as a product, it was relatively accessible through Mexico; it was far easier and quicker to amass in quantities and transport back to the U.S. than the bulk of marijuana, but it was also incredibly riskier, and carried much heavier penalties. But there was always that tantalizing possibility of getting caught when dealing in any of these illicit trades. Easy, fun, forbidden, culpability. It was as if this version of Kit Williams had been scratching and conniving to take control long enough. And so, it did. And Kit simply allowed the morality of it to gradually slide into plausible acceptability, and disappear down the black hole of his own private disillusionment.

  Over the stifling, rough-riding miles and hours on the bus to Huntsville, Kit began to watch the reflection of his face in the windows – along with the reflections of memories of himself traveling the back roads of Mexico. The images were spliced together by some sort of unauthorized editor of his consciousness. Mostly, he was alone. But sometimes he was with Suzanna and the dog.

  The dog. Sam. Kit had purchased the dog from a man on Coney Island who had the questionable distinction of being a "breeder and trainer of dogs and alligators." Kit had read the small ad in the New York Times. Intrigued, and in search of a puppy, Kit borrowed a car and drove the half-hour from Greenwich Village to Coney Island and quickly found the address. It was not far from the aquarium, with a giant hand-painted sign that reinforced the original proclamation: "Breeder and Trainer of Dogs and Alligators." It may have been a converted grocery store; an odd mix of architecture, with dubious stability. Once inside, its smell of fish and wet wood told Kit he was likely going to rescue a puppy regardless of the breed or expense. Nothing healthy could live here long, he intuited. And his lifelong empathy for animals surged.

The room he had entered was filled with cardboard boxes and wooden crates; odd pathways seemed to crisscross it at varying intervals.

"Hello..." Kit called out a bit hesitatingly, leaning into the space without actually walking through it.

"Over here," a rough old voice floated from behind some of the boxes – vaguely in front of him and to his left.

"Looking for a puppy," Kit called back.

"Figured it weren't an alligator," the voice rejoined. "Very few is."

"Could you tell me where you are exactly?" Kit requested, trying to follow the sound of the voice.

"Best wait for me to come git ya'," the voice called back.

Something growled. An unfamiliar sound, definitely not canine. So Kit stayed put as instructed. He could hear footsteps shuffling in the back of the room.

An aged, permanently weather-stained face wearing an old captain's cap over a weary body appeared from behind a pile of boxes marked as once containing books from China. The man walked as if he were completely worn out, rocking from side to side in perpetual pain, a compilation of rusty joints and scars and old wounds, moving on nothing but willpower and need.

"What kind a puppy was you wantin'," he started, not inhospitably, but with no preliminaries.

"What kind you got?" Kit smiled in response, trying to warm the man up.

"Hounds, mostly. Basset hounds today."

It sounded like the daily special.

"Can I see them?"

"Course. Back here."

The man took him through a maze of leaning cardboard and wood, paint cans and rusted signs and other indistinguishable shapes, until they reached a door at the far end of the room; here, they passed into a much more hospitable environment. Warmer at least; drier. Behind a barricade consisting of a duct-taped wooden gate on hinges was a large crate, open at the top, lined with clean blankets and towels and newspapers. It was also lined with five sleeping puppies.

"They're ready to go, seven weeks today," the man stated as if the sale were already made. "All males. The females go quick. Good breedin' stock, them are."

Kit wondered at the competition the man was creating for himself in dog-breeding. But then remembered that it wasn't always basset hounds that this man had to offer. Plus, he was also a trainer of same.

"I hadn't thought about getting a basset hound," Kit stated honestly.

"Then why'd ya' come here?" the man asked.

"Your ad didn't say what kind of dogs," Kit reminded him.

"Long way to come for a dog you're not sure you want," the man countered.

"How do you know how far I've come?" Kit challenged, unable to stop himself.

The man simply looked him up and down. "You ain't from here."

Kit replied: "Not so far away," preferring not to give the man an actual address or the last word.

"You want a dog, Mister? If you do, pick one. If you don't, I got things to do."

"Can I pick them up? I'd like to get an idea of their personalities," Kit replied.

The man started pointing at them one after another: "That one's the alpha. He's pretty strong-willed. Noisy, too. He starts 'em all a-howling. Not good cuz' you livin' in the city an' all. That next one is docile as they come. Rolls over on his back if you sneeze at him. That third one is probably the smartest of the bunch. He figures out how to get out of here 'bout once a day, and can trick the others into allowin' him the biggest part of the dinner. That fourth one is the best for pettin'; he likes his belly rubbed and will let you hold him most all day. And that little one in the corner is the runt. He jes' goes along to go along. He'll do pretty much anything you're gonna want him to. Bit lazy though. So, which one you want?"

Kit was frankly startled by this rather intimate knowledge the man had about these young dogs. Impressed, actually. And he hadn't really considered what kind of personality he was looking for. The puppy was, after all, going to be a gift. A very special gift. In the end, Kit chose the runt. The little one who would just "go along to go along." He paid the man and named the pup "Sam." Sam slept the entire ride back to the apartment, curled up in a shoebox next to Kit on the front seat of the car. Kit was almost home when he realized he had never even asked to see the alligators.

Sam was to be a gift for a woman; a woman with whom Kit was desperately in love at the time, in an equally desperate attempt to get her to love him back; a woman whose name he could not quite remember anymore. A woman who had successfully resisted everything Kit had to offer. *But who could resist a man with a puppy?* he had finally reasoned in a moment of inspiration. Apparently she could. Because she did. Both of them. So Sam had stayed to live with Kit and together they had come to terms with the heartbreak.

Kit couldn't remember a time when he wasn't warmed and comforted by animals. Intrigued by them. In love unconditionally with them, and loved just as unquestioningly by them in return. *The heart of an animal was the safest place you could ever find to deposit your trust,* he had learned from Bruno, the basement-dwelling handyman, not long after Kit and his mother had come to live in their two-story post-divorce Fort Wayne apartment. Bruno helped Kit hide and care for a steady flow of small kittens and mice and chipmunks and birds that Kit found and brought back to the house over the years. Kit's mother would forbid him from keeping any of them, even though everyone else in the house seemed to be aware of the constant flow and flutter below the stairs and no one seemed to mind except Ruth Williams herself. She didn't actually hold a dislike for animals so much as she feared for Kit becoming too attached; although, if pressed, she might not have been able to define "too attached" – in terms of his heart or her own – a fear of diverting his affection from her, perhaps. Despite the fact that the entire household seemed to be in on the secret, it wasn't discussed by any of them, and Bruno certainly never betrayed the trust. There also didn't seem to be a creature Bruno couldn't understand and wouldn't try to help heal if it was sick or broken – including one fragile, deeply troubled little boy. Some of Bruno's successes were quite remarkable, Kit remembered. Only the one failure, he mused. Only the one child he couldn't quite fix. The landlady, Mrs. Blackstone had, at one time, paused to consider Bruno's remarkable healing skills. She had read of those men and women who were escaping from Germany – former doctors and scientists and writers and teachers – forced to leave families behind, coming to America and taking low employment because they could find nothing better, or preferred to stay hidden in safe obscurity. All she could ever discover about Bruno, however, was that he had come from a small German county near the border of Switzerland, where he had lived alone, as a handyman in a small neighborhood apartment building.

There was a slight thud on the prison bus window just then next to Kit's face, and Kit focused his sight onto the widespread wings of a yellow butterfly, caught by the wind, forced into an early demise against the glass. Kit's eyes fluttered closed at the sight of it, in fitful remembrance: The boy Kit and Bruno were sitting on the back stoop of the apartment house. If you sat on the very top step on the far north side, no one could see you from the upstairs windows, Kit had discovered. Kit and Bruno would have many long talks perched there, along with just as many silences of companionship. "When two friends sit together, there is being no words needed," Bruno used to say with his slow German tongue. He spoke the words one at a time, as he painfully translated them in his head, and they seemed to take on extra wisdom and insight to Kit. During one of these times of companionable ease, on a particularly warm summer day, when Kit was halfway between the ages of 13 and 14, a brilliantly painted monarch butterfly landed on the step by his feet. Kit remarked on it in detail to Bruno, whose eyesight continued to fade with the years. The beautiful creature had been incredibly tattered – as if she had escaped a hungry and heartless bird or some thorny beckoning bush with her life barely intact. There were holes ripped out of both her wings; one of them had a torn bit still clinging to it, dragging against the step behind her. One of her legs was broken. Half of an antenna was missing entirely. But still she flew – with grace and strength and wondrous freedom. Together, Kit and Bruno waited as she rested there in all her glorious battered being. And then, on the next breeze to pass by, she sailed away. At some inexplicable inner-urging, in a blurting out of vulnerability, Kit asked Bruno if the older man thought he, Kit, would ever be able to fly free like that someday. And then, just as suddenly, Kit was quite sorry he had spoken such a thought out loud, with no understanding about where it had even come from. But Bruno validated the moment with serious thought and an eventual reply – although an enigmatic one at the time: "Yes, Christopher, you will be flying away one day ... and the holes, they will fly with you. The places that are torn, that are broken, they do not come back to you. But still ... I know ... you will fly."

The prison bus continued to plow through the heat of the Texas afternoon, which was becoming more and more humid the farther north they went. A sudden plethora of insect death-raps, and the resulting smears of colored wings and bodies appeared across the side windows of the vehicle through which Kit was peering. It brought him out of his reverie and streaked his memories with yet another image of yet another window from yet another time out of the past. In this image, he was sitting behind the wheel of a Chevy Blazer, staring through a mucky, bug-filled, front windshield. They were just inside the Mexican border. Sam the dog – fully grown and mid-yawn – was seated next to him on the passenger's side. Suzanna was there, too, asleep in the backseat. It was late into the night and they were getting gas at a no-name roadside station run by a homunculus of a man whose oily shirt proclaimed the name Cletus in large embroidered fanciful script letters, in woeful opposition to the undersized and unwholesome plainness of the man wearing it. Cletus strutted out of the office and up to car in thick-heeled cowboy boots, a pitiful attempt to compensate for his diminutive height. His pockmarked face was accentuated by fat black eyebrows that sprouted in an unbroken yet crooked line across the bridge of his doll-like nose, and enclosed a pair of close-set eyes. Even his ears were tiny renditions. His filthy small hands slammed the cap of the gas tank down onto the bumper of the car, hoping it might leave a dent. The huge ring of presumptuous keys hanging from his belt scratched along the side of the vehicle. Although his voice was childish in pitch, he made up for it with exquisitely foul language, equaled only by his breath. In Cletus' eyes, Kit and Suzanna were longhaired probably drugged-out hippies, and he, Cletus, was heroically obliging by simply filling their tank with gas. When Kit had the ill manners to request that Cletus wash the bug-covered windshield as well, Cletus reacted with all the fury that only the smallest of beings can acquire though a lifetime of dismissive humiliation (both real and perceived). He shook with anger, then ran back into the building and returned immediately waving above him a revolver that appeared to be half the size of his entire body, yelling obscenities. Kit caught a glimpse of this coming toward them in a side mirror, slammed the car into reverse (and Suzanna onto the floor), and red-lined it into the darkness just as he heard the gun explode through the night, a bullet shattering one corner of the unwashed front windshield. It wasn't until their next stop that they realized they had lost a gas cap and Sam had lost part of his tail in the incident. The dog had never even yelped. They sought medical attention for him at the next town, but by then the gunshot wound was healing quite nicely.

  Kit stirred in his bus seat at these flashes of emotion-ridden memory; his face covered by his hand, he couldn't determine if he wanted to laugh or cry. He tried to do neither, realizing how grossly inappropriate either one would be for his current surroundings.

Halfway through the prison bus trip, they rambled into a forgotten, faded gas station, jostling Kit upright into abrupt consciousness; for a confused moment he thought he'd somehow been bumped back in time and began looking for a small man with a big gun. But it was simply a scheduled refueling for the bus and a restroom break for the men. Two-by-two the prisoners were un-handcuffed and escorted by one of the guards off the bus and into the men's room of the station. Each man was also allowed to choose a soda from the convenience store shelves inside. Kit patiently waited his turn. He more carefully took note of his immediate surroundings within the bus: dried leather seats, cracked and gaping up at him; rust-filled scratches on chrome frames; a floor thick with filth and gum and the prints of a thousand shoes, ghosts of prisoners before him, echoes of children transported to school and home in an earlier incarnation. His eyes wandered down the back of the seat in front of him and he noticed small, uncertain letters carved into the metal with ragged effort; someone – a child, perhaps, or an earlier prisoner – trying to leave a mark, a note that they had existed. Kit stared at the letters and they became words. Odd words: *He lives ...* The message stabbed at his memory, but only around the edges of it – he couldn't quite bring it into focus. Then his mind wanted to complete the sentence: *He lives ... under the stairs ... He lives under the stairs ... He lives under the stairs ... but I know he's there ...* It came back to him then. Enveloped him like wet fog. A poem Suzanna had written – a children's story: *"I have a good friend who lives under the stairs, most people can't see him, but I know he's there."* He remembered the opening lines and when she had written them. But, for the first time, sitting there chained to a bus seat in the Texas summer heat, the words rhymed and sang directly at him. They plunged themselves feet-first into his gut. He was nine years old – and it wasn't under the stairs, it was in the alcove behind the refrigerator in the apartment he shared with his mother. That's where the "other Kit" lived. The Kit who had gaping holes in him. And failed his mother. And hated her for it. And loved her with choking desperation. And wanted his father to take his place in her bed. And wished his father was dead. That was the Kit who was different and kept secrets. No one came near that Kit. No one was allowed. He was safe there, alone, under the stairs, behind the refrigerator.

"You coming out?" The guard's voice made him jump. "It's your turn to piss, Williams. Come on."

Kit was one of the last two prisoners escorted off the bus and into the men's room. He was paired with the man who had been sitting behind him on the bus, a man about his own age he noted; most of them had seemed much older or younger. Once off the bus, Kit glanced up at the large lettering stenciled along the length of the vehicle's side; in huge, neon-painted letters it stated in no uncertain terms: PRISON BUS – DO NOT APPROACH. The words seemed to taunt him, somehow. But he didn't know why.

The gas station's main building was comprised of cheap cinder blocks and crumbling mortar, with free-standing metal signs perched around it like modern-day gargoyles, their faces deformed by sun-stroke and rust, yet still promoting with unaccountable optimism motor oil that *"keeps the world running smoothly"* and soft drinks that were *"the real thing."* As Kit stood waiting his turn at the toilet, he became mesmerized by the signs, watching them rock back and forth against the hot, damp wind, squeaking for attention in nightmarish voices. Then, without provocation or even realization, he began to softly sing the popular product jingle that had become a media phenomenon just the year before in 1971: *"I'd like to teach the world to sing in perfect harmony ..."* Unaccountably, the guard joined in: *"I'd like to buy the world a Coke and keep it company."* So Kit started again – at the beginning, and singing all of the verses, in all their sappy sentimentality that everyone seemed to perceive as a "great revealing truth" and had memorized in some sort of version: *"I'd like to build the world a home, and furnish it with love ... Grow apple trees and honey bees and snow-white turtle doves ... I'd like to see the world for once, all standing hand in hand .... and hear them echo through the hills for peace throughout the land..."*

"It's the real thing..." the prisoner's voice echoed around the walls inside the bathroom and out the propped-open door, cracking through the depressing desperation of the moment. He fairly burst through the door still zipping his pants and all smiles: "Hey ... I thought I recognized you. Kit Williams, right? The Kit Williams Trio, right? That's you, man! That's you ... the singer. I thought you looked familiar. Hey, what happened to you, man? I thought you died or got killed or somethin'."

"Yeah, well, apparently not," Kit half smiled but wondered himself why he hadn't died or gotten killed or something somewhere along the way. There had been plenty of opportunities for it.

"You were good, man. You used to be somebody," the other prisoner kept on.

Kit tried to step around him to get to the toilet, without appearing rude or unfriendly. He glanced over at the guard for help, but the uniformed man was also enjoying this recognition of fame that had fallen so far and was now standing so near.

Kit finally dodged and lunged his way to the door and made it inside. His associate prisoner stood with his foot wedged between the door and its frame, barely outside the windowless, airless room, grinning and talking continuously. Kit found it difficult to focus on his now very real need to urinate.

"Yeah, man, you were really good. We used to listen to you all the time. We had every one of your records, man. So what happened to you, Kit? I mean, like, one day you were up there on Ed Sullivan and makin' records and stuff and then you were gone. Where'd you go?"

"Mostly Mexico, I guess," Kit replied literally.

"Do you know The Kingston Trio, man? Do you know Peter Paul and Mary? You used to play gigs with Harry Bellefonte, didn't you? Yeah, I remember that, he's really cool, man. You ever meet Elvis?" The other man's voice became softer, reverent, almost pleading.

Kit sighed deeply. "Sure, a little bit ... well, we shared the same record label for awhile ... yes we did and he is ... and no, I've never had that pleasure," he replied to the often heard questions in the order in which they were asked. But it all seemed to drift over the other man's head, wafting out on the stench of urinal cake and sweat.

Kit was still struggling to accomplish anything in the bathroom when the guard finally took pity on him. The other prisoner was told to back off while Kit tried to turn his attention to productive thoughts. He envisioned water – the sound of it, the feel of it, the sight of it streaming past him.

He envisioned himself on a raft. A raft crossing a river. Like the one from another trip to the backcountry of Mexico with Suzanna and Sam. They had been in the Blazer then, too, and they had come to the banks of a river where they were told they could get a ferry across to the other side, but it wouldn't come cheap – 1,200 pesos, or nearly one hundred dollars. A lot of money, but the only way they could get to where they needed to be and a cash crop of marijuana. The deal was struck and they awaited the ferry; what arrived, however, were two planks of wood somehow bound to two crossbeams of logs, along with two men with long poles. Inexplicably, the Blazer was successfully driven onto the planks – barely tire width – and Kit, Suzanna and Sam were motioned on to it to stand on either side of the vehicle in front of the ferrymen. Sam was put onto the roof of the car. Against all odds and the rules of physics, they were making their way across the river when the men both planted their poles into the soft bed under the water and halted their forward motion. One of the men then demanded another 1,200 pesos – an additional one hundred dollars. Suzanna exploded. She railed at them, raged against the injustice of it beyond all reason. She was wild with a furious anger Kit couldn't recall ever having witnessed from her. Her fists struck out at the shoulders of one of the oarsmen as he ducked and raised his arms protectively over his face and head, trying to retain control of his pole, his balance, and possibly his life. Kit and the other oarsman stood frozen in awe and fear of her, while Sam wet himself – which caused him to begin sliding across the top of the Blazer, toenails screeching in an attempt to regain his footing. A submerged tree was within a few yards of them, its outstretched branches like ghost arms reaching up from hell. A wild turkey was perched within its tangle of bark and lichen, vulture like and portentous. Roused and alarmed by the mind-numbing sounds of outraged curses and toenails against metal, the giant bird flapped its impressive wings with threatening intent, and aimed relentlessly for Sam. The two creatures became one – a heaving mass of fur and feathers, speaking in tongues, rolling and sliding over the hood of the vehicle, thudding onto a corner of the raft, and sinking into the water. The effect was stunning. Suzanna's anger vanished as quickly as it had overtaken her; she moved immediately to help Sam as he attempted to re-board the float, which was by then undulating wildly. The oarsmen joined in the assist, and then resumed poling the craft forward to the other side of the river. No one spoke. No additional money exchanged hands. Sam stopped shaking once on solid ground. The bird could be seen preening in the distance. Kit, Suzanna and Sam drove off into the backcountry in search of marijuana.

Kit peed with relief.

He was escorted from the gas station bathroom into the convenience store of the building where he smiled to no one in particular while he pulled out a Coke from the refrigerated red bin that stood humming and sweating near the door. When he turned to the interior of the room, his eye caught a display of huaraches – the cheap leather Mexican sandals that had exploded in popularity in the U.S. a decade earlier. He and Suzanna both had owned many pairs of them since their trips to and from Mexico began, but now … He looked down disparagingly at the bright pink plastic things still rubbing on his feet. He supposed he would be issued some sort of uniform clothing from the government once he got to the Huntsville prison, but he wondered about shoes. It struck him almost poignantly about the huaraches. To explain their frequent trips across the border, he and Suzanna had used the footwear as their cover story: theoretically buying them for next to nothing in Mexico, and selling them in the U.S. for profit. They were importers, traders in foreign goods. And that part was true – just not that particular product. Kit surreptitiously, fondly, indulgently, rubbed the sole of one of the sandals against his hand. He ran his finger along the raw edges, smelled the chemical residue of its tanning, and he remembered how that near-toxic odor had filled the back of their car and the tiny rundown motel room where they had stayed when they first set up the cover. The small stash of shoes they kept with them was intended to explain the five thousand dollars cash they had stowed away beneath the spare tire of the car, should they be stopped and searched. And he recalled the time they left the cash behind and forgot about it for two days. Having taken it into the motel room with them for safekeeping, they'd taped it to the bottom of one of the bureau drawers. And then they left it there; driven more than 150 miles, stopped overnight, and discovered its absence, half blaming the other for the numbing oversight. But the cash was still there, still taped in place, when they returned the following day. *Toxic gases from the huaraches killing off our brain cells,* Kit rubbed at his eyes and the memory with a strong urge to laugh out loud.

    The first car to stop since they had arrived at the out-of-the-way gas station pulled in, and the prison bus driver walked over to meet it. A pizza brand insignia was prominently displayed on a magnetic sign jutting up from the top of the car. Apparently, lunch had arrived. One of the guards ushered the group of prisoners over to a splintered wooden picnic table with no benches sagging into a brown patch of grass and weeds under the lone tree on the property. The other guard paid the station attendant for the soft drinks.

    As Kit passed the second guard on his way out of the store, he reached down to his feet, took off a pair of huaraches, and handed them to him. He then returned to the display of leather sandals and uncovered the bright pink plastic flip flops he had buried there, put them back on, and shuffled out the door.

    One of the pizzas was topped with mushrooms that were dried up, curling dark at the edges. Seated on the rim of the rotting table, Kit pulled a thick, whole, grey-white slice of mushroom off the top of the pizza between his thumb and forefinger. He let it dangle as he held it up to the sunlight. He turned it slowly back and forth, as if he were studying its veins and colorations. In the process, he caught the attention of the other prisoners and the guards. Without looking at anyone in particular, he said: "Have any of you had the real stuff?"

There was silence at first. The old grey man who seemed to be unaware of anyone or anything else on the entire trip spoke up: "El hongo ... alucinógenos," he slurred out in Spanish.

The prisoner who had recognized Kit in the bathroom then smiled and said: "Oh, yeah ... 'magic mushrooms' – those things that get you high, man."

Kit just smiled and leaned forward, his elbows on his knees, keeping the fungus in front of his eyes, studying it, sniffing it.

"So you're saying you've had them, man?" the younger prisoner pushed the point.

"It was way out in the Mexican backcountry. From an old Anahuac woman – a native. Not just a Mexican – a real native. She didn't speak a word of English, didn't want to. Barely tolerated us gringos. But she liked me, for some reason. She ran a vegetarian restaurant way out there. Couldn't believe it. She gathered and prepared those mushrooms just for me. It was sunrise. Really still, peaceful. Within an hour I was trying to climb a cliff straight up. And I was pushing and shoving and pulling my dog along with me. God, I can still see how hard he was trying to keep up. I actually made it up quite a way – him too." Kit smiled at the memory: "That stuff's not for amateurs."

With great care, Kit opened his mouth, tilted his head back, and flipped the mushroom into the air. It landed squarely on his right cheek, before it fell into the dirt.

The prisoner who was cuffed and seated behind Kit on the bus, the one who had begun the conversations with him during their break, was named Marco. Marco Mancera. He preferred being called Marc, but rarely was. He had been arrested for stealing high-end, very expensive cars, and was not compunctious about it in the least – had, in fact, rather expected to be caught.

Marco was born into a decidedly mediocre family and he carried on the tradition with adequacy if not obvious dedication. He was the middle child of five. He barely earned average grades in school, excelled at no sports, and displayed little aptitude for the arts. Marco did show amazing ability in two areas, however: he could really take a punch, and he could boost any car ever built.

It had been discovered late in life that Marco had dyslexia, which kept him out of Vietnam (a sincere disappointment to Marco) but had created in him a singular gift for aligning himself with others who could camouflage his deficiency – fill in for his needs and substitute for his reality. He saw such a potential in a friendship with Kit, although the exact way in which Kit could be useful was not immediately apparent to him.

Marco readily accepted, almost embraced, his mediocrity. It allowed him to disappear into the background in a chosen profession where this was a definite benefit. And then he made up for his ordinariness by becoming an exceptional "romancer of women" – in his own words, and his own eyes. Happily, one other person shared this perception. Her name was Nina.

"Her name is Nina," Marco said as he leaned across the back of the bus seat in front of him and spoke to Kit in a voice loud enough to be carried through all the attendant noise of the road but that still held a note of confidentiality in it.

"Pretty name," Kit nodded noncommittally, not sure what the comment meant or if he wanted to encourage conversation.

"She's Mexican," Marco continued.

"Ah ..." Kit nodded again.

"I had to win her heart from somebody else. But, man, I am really good at that," Marco grinned without self-consciousness.

"Yes ... I imagine you are," Kit agreed, once again questioning the direction or desirability of this conversation. He turned his attention to the window, thinking this might discourage Marco's continued attempts at engaging him.

"So, you really ate 'magic mushrooms,' man?" Marco abruptly changed topics.

And this one's on me, Kit thought to himself. "Yeah – just like I said. A wonderful old native woman gave them to me. But never again – not for me."

"So, you spent a lot of time in the backcountry?" Marco asked.

"A bit." Kit shifted the chain that attached his left arm to the bar on the seat back in front of him; he resignedly swiveled his body sideways and leaned against the wall of the bus, swinging his leg partially up to the seat bench so he could half-face Marco behind him.

"Man, what for?" Marco asked with an unreadable face.

Kit looked closely at him. "Seriously?"

Marco grinned: "Pot."

"Pot," Kit confirmed with a slight twist to his head.

"So ... did you, like, grow it, man?" Marco lowered his voice a bit with a glance over to the nearest guard.

"Not personally, no. Just made connections with local growers and dealers."

"For friends or market?" Marco asked with understanding.

Oh, what the hell, Kit thought at that point, weighing the advisability of disclosure to this stranger. "We were trying to develop a market," he sighed. "We were just sort of figuring it out."

Over the next half hour or so, Kit entertained Marco with stories about how he had begun working with individuals mostly through chance encounters, buying bits and pieces of field-grown stuff, which was really bad quality and took forever to amass in any kind of quantity. Then, how he had moved to hooking up with farmers – growers – in order to buy several hundred pounds at a time. Before he knew it, he was telling the "romancer of women" about his own head-over-heels encounter with one grower's wife. She was a farm woman, a backcountry farmer's daughter, granddaughter, wife, mother – a woman who had never been away from her village a day in her life and was completely uneducated and unsophisticated, and yet he had been absolutely smitten with her – she owned his heart and he could not say why.

"It's their eyes," Marco had commented sagely. "Those deep, dark, black eyes that see into a man's soul, somehow."

"Whatever it was, she owned my soul," Kit confessed.

"And you wanted to buy stuff for her, right?" Marco understood.

"Yes, exactly. I wanted to buy stuff for her," Kit remembered. "Neither of us spoke the other's language, but I finally realized she wanted a radio. So I bought her the biggest damned radio I could find."

"And ...?" Marco prompted.

"And I never saw her again."

Both men fell silent for a time.

An hour before they arrived in Huntsville, the bus passed a small, private airfield, and the attention of all the men became riveted on the air show taking place there. Old biplanes and other single-engine props were lined up across its acres of open ground; a WWI Vickers Gunbus was pulling in after landing just minutes before; two WWII Messerschmitts were simulating the maneuvers of a dogfight above the appreciative crowd.

Marco pointed to one distinctive aircraft off to the side and exclaimed with great enthusiasm, "Hey ... there's a Sopwith Camel, right? Like Snoopy flies ... Charlie Brown's dog ... in Peanuts!"

"And there's a Morane-Saulnier," Kit said mostly to himself, barely audible, as he turned as far as he could in his seat to catch it before it was too late.

"How'd you know that, man?" Marco asked, impressed once again with his new friend's worldliness and experience.

"It was a French plane made for World War I combat. My mother's French. Her dad actually worked for the company that built them." Kit tried to recall the dusty childhood stories worn thin and fragile over time. He did vividly remember the day that Rene (the distant relative who lived across the hall in the apartment house) had treated him to a similar air show just outside of Fort Wayne for his twelfth birthday. He could still see her seated at her dressing table, dipping her comb into some sort of thick clear gelatin, and then carefully creating stiff long curls in a cluster at the top of her head, securing them with a thousand hairpins; she then repeated the pattern over each ear. He thought she looked as if she had piled sausages on herself, some slipping to each side. He was terribly anxious, fidgeting to be on their way to this tantalizing birthday excursion that he still couldn't believe his mother had agreed to, but he stood in silent awe as she composed her hair. And then, as a final touch, she tucked it almost entirely under a long-brimmed hat designed to keep the sun off the back of her neck. During the show (as she continually held onto her hat to keep it from flipping backwards while she viewed the planes overhead) Rene had spent time talking to Kit about all of the different designs of the planes, of which she knew a surprising amount. She also talked to him about his French grandfather and grandmother, whom he had never met, and their familial home and proud ties to a small town on the outskirts of Paris long before the war. Kit never spoke to his mother about any of this discussion. He never thought to consider why.

"Cool," Marco expressed as the airfield became a distant blur of colored dust. "That was so cool, man. So, can you fly a plane, man?" Marco settled back into his seat after having leaned and craned his neck to see the show through the smeary, wire-filled windows.

"Oh, God, no," Kit replied with feeling. "I guess I thought about it once ... thought about learning. Back in the days of trying to figure out how to get our 'product' out of Mexico and up to New York." He laughed with sudden recall: "But then one time I found myself chasing this little cargo plane down a runway in the middle of the night out in some God-forsaken part of Mexico with the 'policìa' in trucks hot on my butt. Literally – running on foot like a madman after it. It sort of discouraged my enthusiasm." He omitted the part about having his life threatened by a really frightening, very connected, dealer as an adjunct to the adventure. He had been told by the man that he must never speak of this meeting between them to anyone. He wondered if Marco would have counted as "anyone."

"So then what'd you do, man?"

"It was back to cars and ground transportation. But all I had was that bright yellow Chevy Blazer, and it didn't really blend-in well. So I got hooked up with a girl and her brother who sold me a VW camper that had removable seats and interior panels. It could hold hundreds of pounds of marijuana – very concealed. The idea was she and I would swim it across one of the narrow parts of the Rio Grande River from Mexico into Texas. The brother would be there waiting with the van. A couple of trips and the van would be loaded, ready for me to just drive on up to New York."

"Did it work?" Marco asked with sincerity.

Kit closed his eyes, yanked irritably at the chains confining his arms, and slid down a bit in his seat. "What do you, think, Marco? What do you seriously think?"

In his head, however, Kit was remembering how it had almost worked, how it should have worked … and of the one brilliant night when it had all come together. It had been just a week earlier, before the monsoons had come, with all the floods and crippling deluge of water that had arrived so suddenly, so unexpectedly. The girl's name was Maria – at least that's what she told him it was. They called her brother Tony. It hadn't occurred to Kit to not use his real name. But he wasn't as experienced at this as they were.

It was during a dark moon. Maria and Kit had already experimented with river crossing times and depths and difficulty, and varying weights of backpacks in the water. Their clothes had to remain dry, of course, so they swam naked beneath the backpacks. Maria wasn't particularly beautiful; but she had long hair and strong legs, full breasts with dark nipples, and skin that was tanned and looked like honey in the shadows beside the river, and she didn't shave under her arms. She watched him with confidence and a casual disregard for his own naked body and his reaction to hers.

They had chosen a place in the river she knew. It was secluded, not far to the other side. They had brought the marijuana across in the same backpacks Kit had used later. Tony had been waiting at the van, and they had loaded one entire side of the hollow panels and part of the other, enclosing the cargo securely. Then Kit and Maria swam back across the river, with plans to meet up with Tony again the following night to finish packing the van, and to part ways; Tony had already received the money, and Kit would drive the product up north to New York for distribution. What they had not foreseen was the coming storms.

But that night, the water was still quiet and warm, the current soft against them. The sky grumbled at them in warning and intentionality; but Kit and Maria were too absorbed in one another to pay attention to it. Maria had brought a rough towel with her, and she had begun slowly drying Kit's back, when the inevitable happened between them.

His mind drifted back to that very moment of summer heat and crackling lightning. And then farther back. And Mother was drying him after a bath.

Kit sat straight up in the bus seat, cold sweating, face burning, he couldn't breathe. His ears hissed. But his brain didn't have time to create any recognizable feelings, or to fully examine the flashback before it closed the door, retreating out of sight, back to the place where it had crouched behind the "other Kit" – behind the old apartment refrigerator – for years.

With a shuddering jolt, the bus came to a halt, and then crept slowly forward, groaning and creaking, transporting them through the alarming gates of Huntsville State Penitentiary.

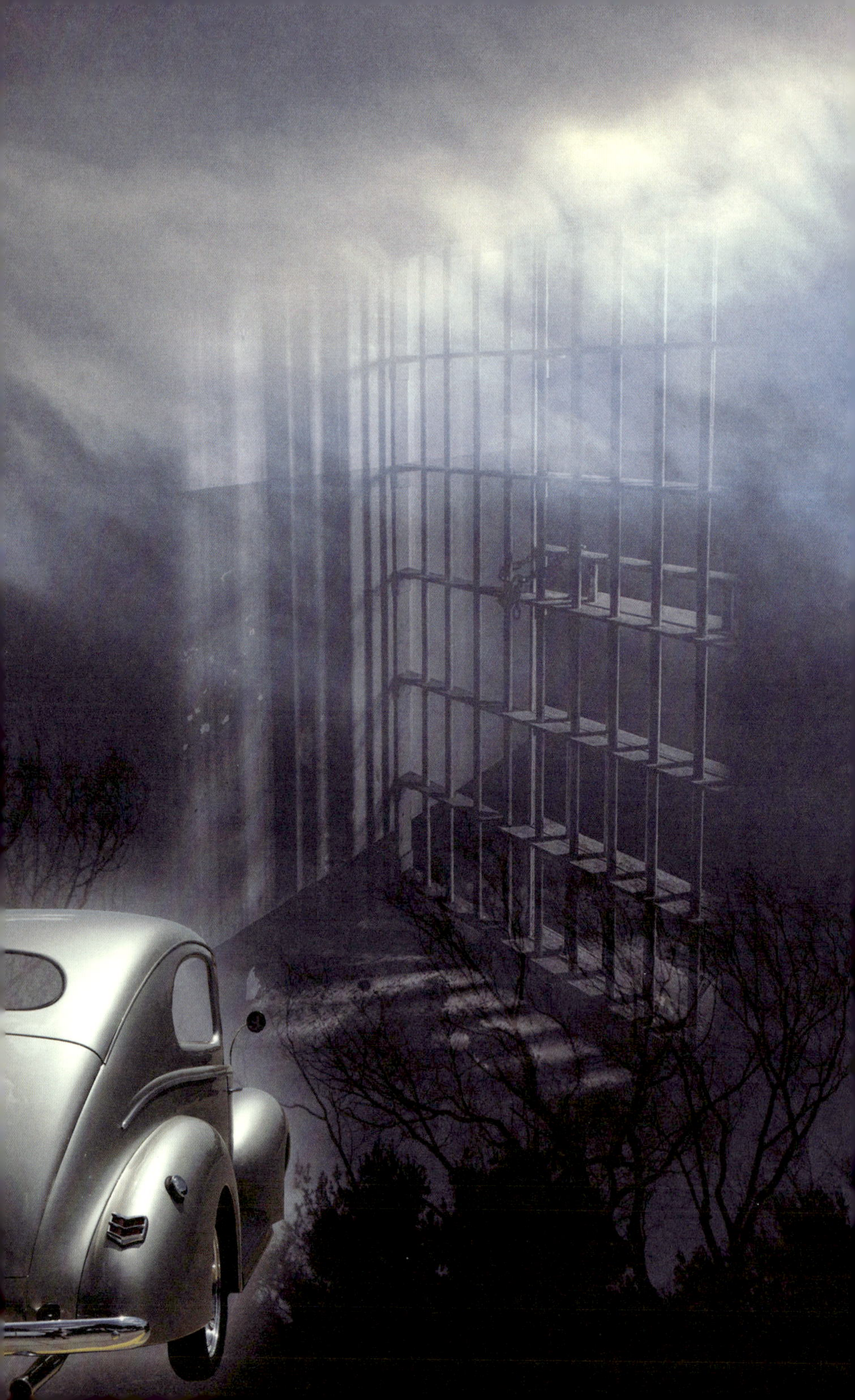

PART TWO

Huntsville Prison.

July 14 - July 31, 1972

As the prison bus pulled through the massive gates of Huntsville State Penitentiary, one of the guards turned and grunted out: "Gentlemen ... welcome to The Walls."

There was no doubt as to why Huntsville Penitentiary was known as "The Walls Unit" – or "The Walls" to its inmates and other intimates. Its massive brick boundaries were ominous, forbidding. They scowled against the sun so that even their shadows appeared impenetrable. The facility had been built in 1849, just a year after Texas had at last torn itself, bloodied and battle fatigued, out of Mexico. For its first nine decades, the penitentiary was barricaded against the outside world with thickset yet pale walls of local sandstone; these enormous enclosures were then encased in brick in 1940, and they now appeared to Kit as raw-red, rough, and hard-baked – not unlike the prisoner hands must have been that manufactured them a generation earlier. Nearly as infamous as its walls was the prison's "death house." Here was where men had been hanged by the neck, or burned with efficiency while strapped securely in the arms of "Old Sparky," and were now poisoned to death by injection into their own arms. Ironically, every prisoner jailed anywhere in the entire area that was completing a sentence or being paroled back into the living world was released through the Huntsville Prison gates – with a spiffy set of donated clothes, a few new dollars in his pocket, and the local bus station just down the street. Kit looked longingly at the beckoning Greyhound sign before it disappeared from tantalizing view on the other side of the prison gates that were closing with formidable finality behind him.

☾

Because of the timing of his arrest, along with the chaotic storms and relentless floods and his resulting transport to Huntsville, Kit was not brought before a judge until the following Monday, July 17th. It was as if Mother Nature herself had already been judging him, with her shifting moods and disquieting moons, her rage of temper and swirling disgust, all the rants and tantrums and disapproval she could gather around her, meant to add to Kit's own sense of instability and precarious control.

It was late in the day and sweltering inside an airless, anxiety-filled courtroom in downtown Huntsville; the decidedly tired and uncomfortable and ill-tempered Judge Harrison Eustace Huston was presiding.

Judge Huston leaned back in his hard-ridden spring-loaded cowhide chair. He slouched low in it and swiveled slowly side-to-side. He listened to the shuffling din that passed for the Texas legal system going on around him. He watched the self-important people; the scared ones, the stupid ones. He tossed a file onto his bench and privately evaluated Kit Williams. Then he swung his left leg up and out from under his robes; he raised his foot high in the air in its handmade, hand-tooled cowboy boot, held it hovering over the desktop in front of him. Heel-first and sledgehammer-hard, he slammed it down on the hardwood surface of the desk. It had the effect of a gunshot. The glass of water placed at the edge of his desk teetered and slopped. Papers scattered. His pen rolled to the floor. Only a couple of elderly, impotent, dust-covered, ceiling fans creaked and dared breathe in the ensuing silence. Both the prosecuting and defense attorneys suddenly came to their feet, hastily buttoning up their jackets, sweat and dignity.

"Sit down counselors," the judge said quietly. "I want to talk to Mr. Williams." He kept his left calf and foot hooked over the top of his desk and looked across the top of his glasses at Kit, who was seated next to his defense lawyer, in front and slightly to the right of the judge's bench. Judge Huston pointed a long reedy finger at his foot propped up in front of him. "How many toes are in this boot, Mr. Williams?" he asked.

Kit's lawyer groaned softly. Looking sideways at Kit, he motioned for him to stand up. Kit stood, but wasn't quite sure what to do or say next. The judge helped him along with a slighted raised voice: "I said, how many toes are in this boot, Mr. Williams?"

Kit began to speak, cleared his throat, and replied: "I want to say five, Your Honor."

"You want to say five," the judge repeated. "You want to say five. Well, Mr. Williams, I'd like to say five, as well. But we'd both be wrong. There are two, Mr. Williams. Two toes are in this boot."

Kit looked over at his lawyer, Steve Silva, a Texas member of the bar called in by Kit's New York attorney to represent him locally. Silva was looking straight ahead, straight faced.

The judge continued: "Do you know where the other three toes are, Mr. Williams?"

Kit slowly shook his head.

"Do you know where the other three toes are, Mr. Williams?" the judge repeated, not changing his tone or inflection.

"Apparently, I do not, Sir," Kit responded.

"In Italy, Mr. Williams. They are in Italy ... left there in 1944 ... in a blood-soaked battlefield ... next to my left knee cap, half of my left buttock, and my entire left testicle." He raised his foot off the bench and returned it heavily to the floor, never taking his gaze off of Kit. Adjusting himself upright in his chair, and then leaning forward, Judge Huston lowered his voice and asked: "And where did you do your military service, Mr. Williams?" He fingered the file folder in front of him.

Steve Silva stood up and said: "Relevance, Your Honor?"

"My courtroom, Mr. Silva. It's relevant if I say it is," the judge responded.

"Of course it is," Silva replied. "But if I may, Judge, perhaps I could relate to you Mr. Williams' unique service to his country."

"Oh, yes, Mr. Silva. I look forward to it."

But the judge did not let Mr. Silva continue first. He did, in fact, spend a great deal of time asking more questions directly of Kit. An entirely different line of questioning. Questions about Kit's understanding of the charges and the proceedings, and whether he was on any drugs at the time, and if he was satisfied with his lawyer. Kit was initially confused, off-balanced, and a bit embarrassed by the inquiries. But then he heard the reality of it, the legality and the justice of it, and something else in the judge's voice even let him hear a sort of kindness in it.

When Judge Huston was satisfied with Kit's responses, he leaned back in his chair and turned a cagy grin back to Steve Silva, and told him he could now continue to explain just how Mr. Williams managed to miss out on serving his country in the military.

Steve Silva, along with everyone in the county, was well aware of Judge "Cannon Ball Harry's" personal prejudice against any eligible man who had not seen active military duty (preferably combat, wounded all the better). The stories of his missing body parts were legend. Silva himself had survived a tour in Vietnam (still fought to survive it most nights), and he begrudged no one who did not have to carry that around with them for the rest of their lives. Perhaps naively, Silva had actually hoped to keep the fact that his client had not experienced combat out of the record. The attorney glanced quickly over to the Judge's clerk, but the man refused to meet his eyes, so he knew there would be no getting around this. The Judge obviously had the facts. He'd have to spin it the best he could.

As Steve began to speak, his Texas drawl became noticeably thicker. He paced a bit behind the table, straightened his chair, motioned to Kit as the story was told. He talked about Kit's college years as a scholarship student studying to become a medical doctor, his heavy musical touring load; and then he introduced The Trio's ambassadorship to foreign countries through President Kennedy's Cultural Exchange program. (Kennedy's name still carried its influence and mystique, even with the judge.) He explained about Kit trying to enlist in the Air Force, but being denied because of his eyesight; and about Kit then trying to serve in the reserves, but how his grueling schedule traveling for his country prevented him from fulfilling that commitment. And how, in the end, it was actually the United States government that decided The Trio was far more valuable in their cultural exchange role than with troops on the ground.

"So President Kennedy himself tapped Mr. Williams for this duty," the judge nodded sardonically. "And where did this cultural exchange take place, Mr. Silva? … And did Brazil need particular convincing of the ideals of democracy? … Yes, Communism is indeed a threat in that part of the world. … But Mr. Williams didn't actually serve in the military now, did he, Mr. Silva?"

"His active service was in the interest of peace, Your Honor," Silva responded, desperately sidestepping the sarcasm.

"Service for peace, my half ass, Mr. Silva. I can just imagine what you've got planned for his defense at trial. Let me guess … drug trafficking for peace."

Kit witnessed it all as if they were talking about someone he never knew, never even met. He felt nothing for this stranger whose life they seemed to be discussing and determining. He wasn't even particularly surprised with the realization – or perhaps it was a personal confirmation – that justice sometimes depended on who you didn't piss off … and truth was only a point of view.

☾

Kit had discovered from Steve Silva that it was Tony, Maria's brother, who had betrayed him. Arrested on a completely unrelated charge, Tony gave them Kit and the VW van and the idea that this was a massive drug distribution operation.

But Steve had prepared a compelling case on Kit's behalf. It was an old law that had allowed for Kit's arrest – one that had been used primarily during prohibition for searching cars without a warrant when time was of the essence and the vehicle could be moved at any moment. That's what they had claimed. But the rains had come – the storms, the flooding, the delays. And the van had sat unattended, unclaimed, for three days. There had been plenty of time for a warrant. And so, he would argue, the old pre-war precedent wasn't applicable, and it was an illegal search and seizure.

Additionally, they had been looking for cocaine or heroine, but all they got was marijuana. And, although any amount of marijuana possession was a felony in Texas, the ten pounds found in Kit's backpack, vs. the forty-two pounds found in the van, could sway the charge and subsequent sentencing from simple possession to possession with intent to distribute.

In the end, Kit was, quite frankly, impressed with Steve Silva's cleverness, his thoroughness, his performance in a courtroom. During their initial consultations, Kit had not felt particularly inspired to confidence by the Texas attorney – especially based on his personal presence. Silva's face appeared much too young for the rest of him. At the same time, most of his hair seemed to be not his own, a disquieting color of melting brown. He smiled too much, showing perfect teeth and emitting a medicinal Listerine-soaked breath. The smile was mouth only, never engaging his eyes. This day he wore an expensive yet ill-fitting suit over a wide-collared white shirt with flaring French cuffs that were secured by huge gold-painted and chipped cufflinks; his tie was knit and flecked with confetti-like metallic bits. His aftershave was too much "Hai Karate" – clashing rather horribly with his antiseptic breath.

And yet, Kit conceded, the man's eyes were cunningly sharp while his voice was educated and quiet and firm. His questions to Kit had been few and pointed, and his instructions were clear. He had also brought Kit clothing for the initial court appearance, advising him against wearing the standard all-white prison attire. And, God Bless the man, he had included a pair of slip-on loafers that actually fit.

What Kit did not know at the time was that Steve Silva also had a strong personal prejudice that he brought with him to the courtroom; his, however carried an entirely different impetus than that of Judge Huston's. Silva's own memory of The Kit Williams Trio dated back to his college days. The group had performed at the university in Illinois where Steve attended and he had gotten in to see them. The room had been packed with the students all seated on the floor. He'd gathered the courage to ask a girl he'd admired from several of his classes to go with him, but she'd refused. She never gave him a reason, she just said "no." When he arrived at the concert he realized he was seated directly behind her, so near he could have touched her shoulder. She was with a group of other girls – all of them vaguely pretty and pretentious and dressed like they

shared the same closet with their little pastel sweater sets
and pleated skirts and black flat-heeled shoes. Something
in him was glad when he saw she had a huge run in one of
her nylons starting near the heel of her left foot; but when
he saw it extended the entire length of her leg, disappearing
up under her skirt, it excited him, and then irritated him.
Throughout the entire performance, Steve tried hard not
to watch the girl as much as he watched the stage. Kit
was the spokesperson for The Trio, and Steve noted how
attentive the girl had been whenever Kit talked – as
enraptured as when he sang, her eyes constantly on him.
The girl was completely captivated. Steve's heart twisted.
He lingered after the concert, watching as the audience got
autographs and gushed over the performers. But Kit never
appeared; he never came from backstage, although the
other two members of The Trio had. The girl and her friends
waited until almost everyone else had gone, and then they
walked back to their dormitory, the girl laughing falsely
and pretending it hadn't mattered that she had not met
Kit Williams. But Steve had known it mattered. And it
pleased him enormously. When Steve got the call from
Joel Menken to represent his famous client in this startling,
destiny-driven situation, it also pleased him enormously.
He would show the girl at last. He would win the case.
And it drove him to developing a very tight and
convincing representation.

Judge Huston proved to be a prejudiced man, but not an incompetent judge; he declared Kit could be freed on bond (albeit excessively high at fifty thousand dollars) and he would have to be assigned a probation officer in New York when he returned home.

As they parted, Silva extended a sweaty hand to Kit and gave him the advice: "Try not to worry, Kit. Our case will hold up. Get your bond money together – and try to raise it all, don't involve a bondsman if you don't have to. You'll be released from custody once it's paid. I'll be in touch."

Fifty thousand dollars. His bond was fifty thousand dollars. It might as well have been fifty million dollars. Where was he going to get fifty thousand dollars? It was all Kit could focus on, repeating it over and over in his head like a mantra as he traveled back to prison from court. Fifty thousand dollars. He remembered when just fifty dollars had seemed like a fortune.

Although Kit would never consider stealing money outright, he was adept at getting what he wanted without paying for it. It was something he had cultivated early in life. One memory in particular stayed with him. And he could still taste the gasoline on his tongue. The fumes filled the back of his throat and burned up into his sinus cavities. He couldn't remember who had taught him how to siphon gas from parked cars. Perhaps he'd seen it in a movie or read about it someplace. But he did recall exactly when the idea hit him that he could get all the gas he needed for his own car without paying a cent for it. It was the day he and his buddies were looking over the new arrivals at Mr. Lucky's New and Used Car Dealership in downtown Fort Wayne. It was a Saturday morning, the summer Kit was 17. Lucky was personally showing a potential customer one of the new Chevys that had recently been delivered to the lot; they walked all around it, touched it with admiration, discussed its features, decided to take it for a test drive. The two older men opened the doors of the car and got in, Lucky pulled a key out from under the floor mat on the driver's side, started the car up, and together they drove away. Kit's friends watched how beautifully the car maneuvered, how quietly it ran, how its chrome glinted in the sun like liquid silver. Kit watched and considered: *That car was unlocked, the ignition key was waiting under the mat, and it had gas in it.* It didn't take him long to determine that this was a fairly constant status with all the cars on the lot, even overnight.

     Siphoning gas could be done quickly, quietly, and relatively undetected; however, separating a car from its other replaceable and often needed equipment – like tires, hubcaps, headlights, batteries, mufflers – required a more complex procedure and, therefore, a more private setting. Kit readily devised a way to take a car off the lot and drive it into a heavily forested area not far from the high school. Safely hidden, he could remove the desired part, exchange it for the one from his own car, and return Lucky's car to the lot before morning. It was typically days before anyone noticed the substitution; sometimes, they never did. One night, Kit determined a need for a full set of new tires. He made his selection; a car well-equipped and easily extracted from the lot, as if he were rustling cattle in an old western. How the police got wind of it, Kit never knew; but he was already tucked well away in the woods, and there was no moon that night, and so it didn't stop him from taking the tires – it only prevented him from returning the borrowed car back to the lot. He worked with alacrity, in the pitch dark, as he watched the flashing lights and listened to the sirens of two police cars passing on the main road almost within shouting distance from him. As far as he knew, that car of Lucky's was still sitting there up on blocks, now rusted and rotting and sinking farther and farther into decay, abandoned, wasted, somewhere out in the woods near the old high school. All for fifty dollars worth of tires.

The gates of Huntsville Penitentiary clutched at him as he passed though them once again on his return from court, and Kit wondered if perhaps pieces of himself were also still sitting next to that old stolen car – rusted and rotting and sinking farther and farther into decay, abandoned, wasted, somewhere out in the woods in the dark – or perhaps just behind the refrigerator in the alcove at the edge of his mother's kitchen.

☽

The Huntsville prison cellblocks were hard, institutional, impersonal, and crowded. Beds were bunk-style, and made Kit think of cement-walled dormitories in an unfortunate boarding school – almost Dickensian, but a hundred years later and lacking kindly old uncles. There was no kindness about Huntsville Penitentiary. The best one could expect was tolerance. Kit was tolerated by the currently established residents in his block, but only after they had defined some initial ground rules.

It began with the designation of which bed was to be his. This was not decided by any official assignment – it was determined by the men themselves. Like much of the internal culture of the place, this seemingly unimportant element of life was taken quite seriously; it represented status and respect and a certain standing within the community. Kit was placed into a cell for four men, two of whom were already living there. He was deposited into it like nothing more important than a milk bottle rattled into a metal container on a morning doorstep, replacing the empties just taken away, and the other two men looked him over quite thoroughly with open curiosity. One circled him like a dog; Kit listened for him to sniff, then waited, watching.

Kit Williams was indisputably attractive; an ivy-league, boy-next-door, upper class attractive. It was an appearance that was a perfect match for his profession in music, folk singing, college campus performances, clubs, tours, posters, album covers, TV appearances. It was a look perhaps less suited to prison. He was not tall but fit and carried himself with an athletic ease. He was fair-haired, brown eyed, smooth cheeked, light skinned. His eyes were widespread and clear. His nose was short over a full lower lip, good teeth and muscular jaw. He was "every mother's son" with a quick, bad-boy smile. Even in his thirties, he could give the impression that his father's lawyers would be there any minute with plenty of bail money. It was an image that was woefully deceiving, unfair, and often disserving to Kit. Fortunately, there was also an energy to Kit that was nonthreatening, nonjudgmental, intelligent, open, worth trusting – but stopped just short of passivity or vulnerability. And so he passed their mostly intuited inspection. Kit walked over to the nearest set of beds and started to sit on the lower bunk. One of the men shook his head, however, and then nodded to the upper level. Kit smiled and lifted himself up to it easily and amiably, instinctively understanding the politics of it.

  A potentially much more serious negotiation, took place the next morning in the shower room. Kit learned quickly that there must be no eye contact, no conversation, no lingering next to anyone – unless you were willing to follow through with a more significant connection. Fortunately, the inmate who taught Kit this lesson was grudgingly tolerant of the newcomer and decided to let the misunderstanding pass. It was a rare grace to be granted.

  The third rule that Kit was obliged to observe was relative to noninterference in a fight. It was made clear a few days after his arrival. A new inmate was delivered to the cell, a transfer: he was Marco Mancera. At first, Kit was rather pleased to see the fellow bus prisoner with whom he had become acquainted on the long trip up to Huntsville, the self-proclaimed "romancer of women." But before Kit could even acknowledge him, Marco was down.

Apparently, Marco had also been recognized by one of his other cellmates – recognized as the "romancer of the wrong woman" in some former time and circumstance; the "romancer of another man's woman."

The cuckolded cellmate was named Santiago. Kit was unsure if this was his first or last name, but it was the only one he ever heard used. Santiago had been in Huntsville Penitentiary for slightly longer than two months: a short enough time to still vividly remember all the faces and names and wrongs he'd suffered on the outside, but well into the stage of compounded frustration and boredom and fantasies about what was transpiring on the other side of the wall while he was trapped inside its confines. He was also a bully. Not terribly bright nor a particularly good fighter, Santiago was, instead, mean and deceptive. He saw Marco coming, turned his face away so Marco could not recognize him first, waited until the guard was out of sight, and then attacked the unsuspecting man from behind. Marco had the disadvantage weight-wise and was caught terribly off guard, but he reactively engaged his talent to lean away from a punch even as it was being delivered. He hit the ground immediately, curling into a position of least exposure, providing the most protection over anything vital. Seeing his opponent floored and nonresistant, Santiago let loose with several quick punches to Marco's back and arms and legs, followed by one half-hearted kick. He spit in Marco's general direction, swore hoarsely in guttural Spanish and walked away, puffed up, stiff legged, shaking the sting from his hands, but apparently vindicated with this single strike.

Kit's immediate desire had been to jump into the fray. It usually was. Yet he never knew why. It appeared as if he were defending the brutalized, the victim – when, in fact, it was simply a need to become a part of it. Something drew him toward the energy of the thing – the anger, the pain, the loss of control. Even the cruelty and baseness of it compelled him. He was always surprised afterward, couldn't understand the reason for his actions, if there was any reason to be found. It was, perhaps, the "other Kit" who was lured into the moment, the fierce emotion of it. There was simply a deep, blank chasm between himself and reality during those moments of compulsion. On this occasion, however, the remaining cellmate – an older man by the name of Diego (first name or surname, also unknown) – prevented Kit from entering into the confrontation. Diego never actually said anything. He caught Kit's eyes and intent, there was a slight movement of his head, the barest motion of his hand, but the warning was unmistakable. And then the altercation was over almost in the same moment it had begun. The air still crackled, but it was cleared.

☾

It was five days into Kit's imprisonment, and he was still awaiting word about his bond money, knowing Suzanna was doing all she could and feeling the guilt of that. But the only other emotion of which he was barely conscious was hearing the disappointment in his mother's voice when he spoke to her on the phone. To everything else he felt nothing. No fear, no apprehension, not even any real sense of confinement. It was as if he were watching someone else live the experience. Someone he didn't know.

Within the prison there was no freedom and yet too much of it. The men were regimented in action and disregarded in thought. They were under guard, under rules, under containment – and yet they were beyond the law, governed by their own codes and culture not recorded on any official books but rigidly enforced. Kit tried to give himself some sort of reality to cling to, some personal subtext to his existence, and so began each morning with a sequence of physical exercises: pushups, sit-ups, leg-lifts, running in place. There was no formal workout room or equipment at the facility; so Kit created his own space and routine, which aroused much snickering amusement from his fellow prisoners as well as the guards, and somehow added an odd, subliminal, element of satisfaction to himself.

Kit didn't remember when physical fitness became a part of him. Perhaps it had started with his daily elementary school runs from home – his first practical application of separating himself, creating an alternate reality. It had then filled his time and consciousness during high school – still running, but this time on a track and with recorded times and shining awards and girls to impress and a coach to manipulate him and his mother to watch him. And there was Jacob – and Jacob's footsteps always pounding just behind him. Their coach called them "salt and pepper."

Kit Williams and Jacob Jackson learned early that skin color had nothing to do with life and everything to do with life. They were in the second grade when they began running side-by-side, racing each other – on the playground, to their respective homes and back, and to and from the general store Jacob's family owned. They were perfectly matched in size and skill and in the joy of running. They talked about being different colors; they rubbed at each other's arms and looked behind each other's ears and in each other's mouths and couldn't really tell where the color started and stopped. They thought each skin had distinct advantages and attractiveness and had the exact same feel to the touch. So one day, they decided that they would simply take turns: one would be Black and the other White for a specified time, and then they'd trade. Neither of them could discern exactly how this transition might be accomplished, however. So they posed the question to their teacher, in front of the entire class; and someone laughed, and everyone laughed, louder and louder, and the two friends were sent to the principal's office in tandem confusion, embarrassment and disgrace. Notes were sent home to their parents. Kit's father was already drunk for the night, his mother said she preferred not to discuss it, and Kit was made to eat his dinner alone in his room. Kit refused to ask Jacob what had happened at his house. But sometimes a shared, heart-wrenching humiliation can bond children together in a way no other experience can. And so it was with Kit and Jacob. It was Tuesday, March 23rd, 1943. It was the same day Jacob's older brother was killed in action in the Pacific. When the news reached his family a few days later, Kit held Jacob's head while he cried out behind the garage, and pledged to be Jacob's replacement brother – in heart and in spirit if not in skin.

Although the boys were nearly identically matched when it came to their running skill, by the time they both joined the track team in high school, something always seemed to hold Jacob back, kept him stepping on the edge of Kit's shadow but no closer. It was always Williams, first place, Jackson, second place. Always. Both were naturals, both excelled at the quarter mile. One difference was that Jacob had at least five family members sitting faithfully in the stands at every meet cheering them on, while Kit's mother sat quietly, composedly, alone. Another distinction was that Kit never failed to throw up after a race, while Jacob stood quietly holding a wet towel over his friend's head. When they were juniors, still competing in the same 440-yard dash, the boys decided they would bring drama and focus to an especially high-profile event by clasping hands and crossing the finish line triumphantly together. Their coach became aware of the plan and threatened to bench them both. It was at the end of this race that Kit turned to grin at his close friend as he always did just before inching away from him for the win. But, this time, instead of hearing Jacob's footsteps solidly behind him, they were at that very moment passing him. For the first time running against Kit, Jacob won. Thereafter, Coach kept Jacob in the 440 and moved Kit to the half mile, where he continued to empty his stomach after each race, but he held his own wet towel over his head.

In the autumn of 1955, when Kit and Jacob were college freshmen, both on scholarships – Kit at Stanford and Jacob at Texas Southern University – Jacob insisted on hitchhiking home for Thanksgiving to save his parents the cost of a bus ticket. He was picked up by the wrong person, murdered, and left in a stand of trees at the side of the road just inside the Texas state line. Skin color had had everything to do with life.

"Hey," Marco's face appeared upside-down over Kit in the midst of a sit-up.

"Hey," Kit acknowledged.

"I want to ask you a favor, okay?" Marco inquired with his always-ready smile and never-wavering attitude.

"Okay."

"I want you to help me write a letter."

"To Nina?" Kit stopped his exercising and wiped his face on his arm.

"You remembered my Nina!" Marco grinned.

"Was she perhaps Santiago's Nina before she was yours?" Kit ventured, having witnessed the beating.

"Of course. I told you I had to win her heart away from someone else … and that I am very good at that."

"Yes, yes you did," Kit conceded. "So why do you need my help in writing her a letter?"

"Oh … man, you know … the words don't come like they should when I try to write them. Whispering them in the dark, yes … writing them on paper … no. What do you say, man? You'll do it, yes?"

Kit hesitated for a moment: "Sure. What the hell."

Kit and Marco were required to go to the library to write the letter under supervision. Once they were seated across from each other at a table in relative privacy, Kit picked up the pen and positioned the paper in front of himself to begin writing. Marco had clarified that Kit was to do the actual writing as well as help construct the content. The two men stared quietly at the blank paper for a bit. Then at each other. Then back at the paper. Finally, Kit began writing:

Dear Nina .... He stopped, looked expectantly at Marco. Both remained silent.

How are you? Marco began dictating. *I am fine.*

Kit didn't write any of it down. "Sounds like you're writing to your grandmother, Marco."

"I know," Marco agreed. "So – you tell me what to say."

"I don't know what you want to say. I don't even know the woman," Kit countered.

"Okay ... how about: *Dear Nina – I miss your smell...?*" Marco tried.

"Your smell? I miss your smell? What the hell, Marco, now it sounds like you're writing to a horse. I know what you mean – but, come on, you've got to say it with more class than that. Maybe you could work up to that sort of stuff. Maybe you could just start with *I miss you.*" And Kit wrote it down.

Marco leaned forward, looked at the writing upside down and began dictating again: *And I miss Skip, too.*

Kit wrote that down as well, as he asked, "Who's Skip?"

"Skip's her dog, man. He's only got three legs ... and he kind of skips when he walks. So that's what she named him. Skip. Skip's a good dog, man."

Nina had taken Skip in to live with her when she found him injured and struggling along the side of the road near the restaurant in Laredo, Texas, where she'd been waiting tables and tending the counter six days a week for a little longer than eleven years without missing a day. Skip's leg couldn't be saved, but the dog didn't seem to mind. So Nina didn't either. She felt a similar type of alignment when she met Marco. Nina was not at all fond of her former boyfriend, Santiago, even while she was dating him. But Santiago had that kind of "outlaw" attraction about him that always drew her in at first. He was undeniably good looking, but bad news. When Marco walked into the restaurant, Nina knew right away that he was the one she really wanted. She saw something worthy within his mediocrity. She also sensed that she needed to let Marco think it was he who did the choosing, and that he had actually "won her away" from Santiago. Nina understood the egos of men. She was always more intuition than education or even intelligence. Nina had a rare gift for being able to read people as soon as she met them; she felt their energies, knew their hearts regardless of how they perceived themselves. She was genuinely compassionate, with never a thought to her own benefit; generous and good humored, yet rarely taken advantage of. She had eyes that were deep brown, almost black; hair that was thick and strong and so dark it shone blue in the sun. Her face and body were comfortable with themselves and the rest of the world. Nina was an easy person to be around.

    Kit stared down at the library tabletop in front of him. It was old wood, stiff and dry from time and use and sweat and indifference sinking deeply into its veins; stained a dark, flat, angry shade of brown, it looked rather like coffee boiled too long in a glass pot, and was made cheap with too much varnish. Somehow it reminded him of his mother's dressing table. And, somehow, in the silence of the room and with the unconscious caress of his fingertips, the library table began to fade under his touch, taking the present moment along with it. In its place was a memory strong with the smells of sweet face powder and lipstick wax and freshly laundered handkerchiefs and French perfume. *Vol de Nuit.* His mother's scent was always *Vol de Nuit.* Everything about her smelled of it, he remembered, even the inside of her underwear, mixed together with other vague yet distinct odors of a woman – strange, intimate, confusing. A slur of it reached out to him from the laundry hamper in the bathroom corner whenever he lifted its lid to deposit his own soiled clothing on top of hers.

I miss the warm, familiar scent of you, Nina, Kit suddenly wrote in the letter. And Marco approved.

Kit was lying on his back staring upwards in the semi-dark. The cement blocks over his bunk seemed to be moving, closing down on him, shifting side to side. The cellblock was quieting for the night, but his mind was still thrashing about in time and place. The memory-saturated scent of his mother's dressing table was clinging to the back of his nose and throat. It was as if he had touched it all again. And she would smell it on him. And she would know that he had been looking through her things. She would know about him finding the letter.

Without discretion or pity, or even his awareness, sleep and his subconscious dragged Kit down into the darkness and decades of time. He was barely 13 years old, it was ten days before Christmas 1949, and he was searching for hidden Christmas presents. His mother had gone out for the evening; Rene, from across the hall, was checking in on him periodically. Kit anticipated at least thirty minutes available to him for his pre-holiday ritual of trying to discover the gifts he would be receiving. More often than not, he found them, but was able to act surprised on Christmas morning all the same, enjoying the delight on his mother's face. This year, he had a serious desire for a portable record player – one that would play both $33 1/3$ and 45s. And he wanted baseball cards.

All of the logical places had been gleaned to no avail. He stood in the bedroom and stared at his mother's dressing table and then her dresser. The latter had larger hiding options. It was an imitation Chippendale-style highboy perched on four curved legs; each of its deep drawers had pulls attached at both ends – oval metal backplates with suspended half-moon rings that swung easily and made a tinny tapping noise whenever they were jostled, even if the floor was simply vibrated near them. Their unmistakable sound never failed to wake him on nights when his mother came in late and carefully prepared herself for bed. He always pretended to stay sleeping. Sometimes he raised his eyelids a slit to watch her moving about the room in the diffused light ghosting in from the bathroom. She never turned on the bedroom light, never wanted to disturb him. He watched her outline, moving in and out of the shadows, like on a movie screen. He found himself staring at her breasts as she brushed her hair and he closed his eyes as tightly as he could, but it never seemed to be tight enough. He listened to his breath. And then she would slide into the bed they shared, smooth and quiet, almost secretively. Lifting the covers, she brought in a chill that seeped into the private warmth he had built up around himself. The mattress was old, the springs were worn and broken, and he had to grasp onto the edge of it to keep himself from rolling into her.

    That night, during his search for the gifts, the sound of the metal dresser drawer pulls rang out so loudly at his touch that he was sure they would alert Rene to his illicit activities, even though she was across the hall and there were two closed doors between them. Kit felt a wash of guilt hot under his cheeks as he pulled the bottom drawer open. Here were his mother's sweaters and belts and winter scarves and gloves. But there were no hidden Christmas surprises among them. He considered stopping then, but he didn't. The next drawer up was filled with slips and brassieres and nightgowns; her scent was especially strong in this dark place. His hands worked along the edges and under the silky material; he felt paper, a thick envelope. He pulled it out from its hiding place. It had her name on it in handwriting he didn't recognize. He didn't like her having secrets. He let his fingers lift the flap and glide the pages out of the envelope. Kit had never read a love letter before, but he knew what this was. It was aching, pleading, vulnerable. It filled him with shame and it wouldn't let him put it down. It was intimate and revealing and made his hands shake. It said: "I want you, Ruth" – and other things he didn't want to know. And it was signed: "With all my love and desire, George." She was with George now.

Rene opened the door to the apartment and Kit shoved the envelope back under Ruth's scented, personal, private things; he carefully slid the drawer closed, covering the ring pulls with his hands to silence them, and then he turned away from it.

By midnight, Kit was bathed and in bed but had not slept. When his mother crept quietly through the door, he was lying on his side with his back to her; he closed his eyes and kept his breathing even and shallow. That night, however, she came and sat on the side of the bed next to Kit; she turned on the bedside lamp, and began rubbing his back. When he made sounds as if he were being roused from sleep, she apologized for waking him, and said she had something important to tell him. Kit rolled to his back.

"George Bassington asked me to marry him tonight," she said, not so much to Kit as she did to the floor next to her feet.

Kit remained silent.

"I told him, 'no'," she said. "I told him I had you to consider, and that I thought this might not be the best thing for you, and so I said 'no'."

"Okay," Kit replied. He rolled back onto his side again.

Ruth changed into her nightgown and hung up her clothes with particular care. Then she went into the bathroom, quietly closing the door behind her, and let the water run cold over her wrists and hands. Returning to the bedroom, she turned out the lights and eased herself into the bed behind her son. She wanted to draw him nearer, but his muscles were taut; he was clinging to the edge.

Ruth lay awake all that night trying to imagine what her son was feeling about her and her sacrifices for him. Kit had promptly fallen asleep trying to imagine where his mother had hidden the record player. And in January of 1950, George Bassington moved to Indianapolis trying to forget them both.

Kit awoke to the realities of his present-day imprisonment with a vague sense of relief.

At breakfast that morning, he sat across from Marco. Perhaps governed by nothing more than basic nature, Marco seemed to abhor a vacuum and began a conversation with Kit in a confidential tone – yet loud enough that it would be sure to carry a few seats down the long table to his left and to the ears and ego of his fellow prisoner and personal oppugner, Santiago.

"I had this dream about Nina last night," Marco grinned widely. "Must have been that letter I wrote to her. Man … it was a good dream." He went on to share some of the more explicit details.

Santiago stood up suddenly, lunged down the side of the table, and grabbed Marco by the collar, pulling him backward and leering menacingly into Marco's ever-smiling face; he grabbed a fist full of Marco's hair, wrenched his head sideways and spit directly onto Marco's ear. A guard yelled out a warning and required Santiago to relocate himself to another table. Marco's humor never faltered, and he wiped the other man's spittle from his ear with a paper napkin as he repeated: "It was a good dream, man." He then went on with his breakfast as if nothing had happened, looking over at Kit and asking: "How about you, man? You dream about any of your women last night?"

"Any of my women? *Any* of my women?" Kit was dismayed by Marco's image of him and assumptions of manhood. "As a matter of fact, I dreamed about Christmas as a kid," he responded, "and trying to find my presents before Christmas morning. Actually, I was trying to find a record player that I got one year."

Marco thought back to the mediocre Christmas gifts in his own youth: a pair of pants, socks, some candy or coins. "So, was that record player the best Christmas present you ever got?"

Kit considered the question. "No, Marco, there was one better." Kit set his fork down, leaned in, his elbows on the table, and never gave a thought to the potential disparities between his own upbringing and that of young Marco's. He continued, "The best present I think I ever got – as a kid – was the year I turned 17; that would've been about 1953 … I was a junior in high school anyway. My birthday's just a couple of weeks before Christmas, and that year I got my first car – a 1940 Chevy coupe – it was kind of a metallic blue. My mom bought it from a friend of hers where she was working at a bank. That was an awesome Christmas. God, I loved that car."

"You still have it, man?" Marco wanted to know. "It'd be worth some serious money by now. Man, you should have kept it," he responded to Kit's shaking head.

"It was pretty cool even back then," Kit remembered. "I had already put together a singing group and we used that car to get to some of our first gigs. And every cent I made went right back into the car – for insurance and, you know, other expenses …" his voice trailed away (for some reason, Kit could not recount to Marco about the supply source at Mr. Lucky's New and Used Cars). Kit continued: "I remember it was a week or so before I was allowed to drive it, though – because of the weather. Longest week of my life … well, before now, anyway. It was December in Fort Wayne, Indiana – so it was cold. There was already some snow on the ground; but this particular year it was also really wet and foggy – and it just hovered around freezing all the time. So everything was coated in a layer of ice. Trees and bushes, the ground and the snow – porches, sidewalks, roads – everything. Ice crystals crusting over every surface it touched; really pretty, but treacherous. Day after day, the fog would come back in and settle down on everything, and the moisture in it would freeze solid into a fresh coating; it was very eerie and sort of unreal. My mom wouldn't let me so much as drive around the block. School was closed. So I'd just go out and sit in that car for hours. I'd wrap up in this old blanket, go sit in the driver's seat, in the fog, play the radio…" his voice stopped, caught in the memory. "It was something like eight days before the streets had thawed enough for me to get to actually drive the damned thing."

    Marco nodded as if he understood, but then said: "My first car was a maroon 1952 Hudson Wasp, two-door convertible, and it came from the corner of Park and Salinas Streets in Laredo – near the old city park. I was 15 years old and it was my first solo boost." He reported it with unbridled pride.

    Kit laughed out loud with sudden insight into the irony of the moment and the two stories.

    "What?" Marco grinned in misunderstanding. "I didn't get caught."

    Just then, an ear-numbing buzzer sounded, requiring everyone to stop eating immediately and move on to their daily work detail.

☾

All of the residents of Huntsville Penitentiary were expected to work in some area of the prison, regardless of their sentencing status. The warden was a man named Horatio Bolin and he was an ordained minister, so all things relating to repentance and redemption received priority and personal attention in his prison. He singled Kit out to be assigned to the prison chapel and to sing in the choir. The work itself was light and Kit was a little disconcerted at how good it felt to be singing again – even if it was a church choir and he was a proud practicing unbeliever. Well, it wasn't his religious belief that got him this gig anyway, he reasoned; it was simply his former fame and an inherent talent. Over the next week, however, Kit would learn a great deal about the unpredictability of both fame and talent. And one of the lessons would involve a ghost.

In the preceding decade, Kit Williams and The Trio had toured the country from coast to coast, and many other countries around the world, gathering fans and followers and fame; their recordings were consistently on the charts; their concerts were sold out; they were in demand as a group and recognized as individuals. But in Huntsville Penitentiary, such worldly fame meant nothing. There were, in fact, only two notable current residents within that self-contained, self-defined existence – and neither of these residents was even living. One famed presence was a pair of sunglasses once owned and worn by actor Steve McQueen during the filming of the movie "The Getaway." They were given (by him personally, it was always recounted) to an inmate who had been an extra in the few scenes that had actually been shot at the prison in February of that year; the sunglasses had only been there for four months – with another 14 months to go on the recipient's sentence. The other most famous presence had been there much longer. It was the ghost of native American Kiowa Chief Santana, imprisoned nearly a century earlier. He had eventually escaped by suicide – jumping from a second-story window of the prison hospital. He had served a total of six years behind The Walls, after two questionable convictions. And his body had been held captive another 90 years in the prison cemetery, until it had finally, justly, been released back to his people in 1963. His ghost had been weeping and walking the halls for nearly a hundred years by the time Kit Williams would encounter him.

  Warden Brolin himself verged on fame and had obtained the nickname "The Roaming Reverend" due to his penchant for walking the halls of the entire institution at random and unannounced, showing himself suddenly outside of cell doors in every block, as well as in the mess hall, the hospital, the laundry, the library, even the shower room. He also quoted scripture fluently; he had the entire Bible practically memorized by the time he was 21 and never hesitated to call on its teachings and condemnations to encourage or chastise or simply ambush the recipient. At 6-foot-three, and more than 275 pounds, The Roaming Reverend had cowed even some of the most intrepid and arrogant criminals with his imposing and startling appearances and furious recitations. Sunday services were held in the chapel both morning and evening, and Warden Bolin regularly attended both. Although he didn't preach, he did present the scripture readings with warm interpretation and a terrible passion in his voice that rose and fell impressively, reminiscent of tent revivals – a culture into which he had been born and raised.

The chaplain at Huntsville was almost as famous as the warden. She was a woman by the name of Mary Louise Locke. Before coming to the penitentiary, The Reverend Mary Louise Locke's background was somewhat sketchy and the subject of much speculation within the prison community. She had earned some rather widespread awareness simply by being one of only two women who worked "behind the walls" (the other woman was a nurse in the prison hospital). But among the inmates themselves, Chaplain Locke was most renowned and respected for some of her more mysteriously acquired abilities: it was reputed that she could throw a grown man ten feet in any direction and put a choke-hold on him that would cause him to fall unconscious within seconds (she could kill him in the same length of time if she wanted to, the rumor went). Less impressive to her flock was that she could speak three languages and play a variety of musical instruments. There was a great humor in her, a kindness in her face, and a forgiveness in her theology for just about anybody who was truly repentant. Her sermons made sense and were not too long. All the men were comfortable around her, and she with them.

The music Kit was to perform that Sunday was an a cappella solo backed by the choir. From the first rehearsal, Kit felt humbled by the quality of voices Chaplain Locke had assembled in her choir, and was oddly gratified to be a part of it. He had no idea such talent could be locked up in a place like Huntsville. When he said as much to the chaplain, she responded: "You'd never imagine the talent shut away behind these walls, Kit. There is a painter in one of the cellblocks who can, in a just a few strokes of color and line, take your breath away with the beauty of a world he's lived in for less than half his life: 27 of his 48 years have been spent behind bars. And I've been helping another man with a book manuscript; it's raw and base and the most brilliant writing I've ever read. I didn't know the human soul could fit on paper the way he does it. He takes one-dimensional words and breaks them apart and then puts them back together into something that will punch you straight in the stomach or heal your heart. And you think these men's voices are good – the voices you've got singing with you right now? Kit, you should have heard some of those who have already served their time and moved on. And don't even get me started on the piano player who got paroled last year. I try not to get too attached," she shook her head and smiled.

"Then I'll try to live up to your expectations, too," Kit said, but he couldn't make himself return her smile.

Following the evening service on Sunday, Kit helped Chaplain Locke gather and re-stack the hymnals and prayer books and he lingered a bit for her companionship and a comfort he was unaware he needed. When he left her company, the corridor was concrete-damp and shadow-dark. Even in the midst of the Texas summer heat, the halls of the prison could be chilled with trapped air that seemed years old, aching with stale sadness. It's what Kit felt first – until the dank, wet cold lay heavily across his exposed neck and arms. It stank like men's sweat from fear and unwashed garments. Kit was suddenly overwhelmed with a sense of pending doom and violent grief. He heard the weeping behind him – turned and saw nothing, then vapor, then Chief Santana himself. It was like a water reflection or someone seen through fog. Kit couldn't draw a breath – was almost afraid to breathe in the air emanating from the presence. The footsteps then came; not as hard-soled shoes, but with the soft shuffling of old bare feet against cement floors. Kit hardly recognized his own voice as it tried to call out, whispered, failed, and faded into the mist.

The vapor and cold dissipated as suddenly as they had come. And Kit suspected the ghost had come because of him – something to do with him. But exactly what eluded him.

☾

By the end of the second week, Kit had been in touch with Joel Menken and Suzanna in New York by phone and had met with Steve Silva a couple of more times in person.

As hoped, Suzanna had managed to raise the entire amount of the assessed bond money, as well as at least a beginning on the legal fees. She had called in every favor owed to both Kit and herself. She had signed promissory notes. She had taken up collections. She had closed out every bank account and charged the maximum on every credit card. She sold most of her art and books and some of her furniture and the pearls her great uncle had given her for her high school graduation. Kit's mother, who owned nothing of real value, cashed in her small life insurance policy to add to the total. Kit was overwhelmed with humiliation as much as gratitude, and he tried to imagine how he could pay it all back. But then, for Kit, everything else receded behind a black, bitter, unforgiving anger when Suzanna told him about the late night call she had received from his dad, Joe. Suzanna had thought Joe was contacting her to see how he could help his son; instead, he was asking her to give him some of the money she had raised for Kit. Kit's outrage was practically tangible and was full of old scabs and denied reality. It reeked of a lifetime wasted in disappointment – like walking home alone in the dark when no one came for him, and receiving an award while no one watched; like cold Christmas dinners and unwrapped Father's Day gifts; like shivering in the stands at a baseball game sitting next to a drunk and being too young to leave and too frightened to stay. Kit would never speak to his father after that. Less than a year later, Joe Williams was found dead, alone, underneath an overpass in downtown Indianapolis. In his pocket was an un-cashed check for one hundred dollars from Suzanna.

☾

On July 31st, 1972, Steve Silva was reenergized; he washed his hands and resettled his hair in the men's room just outside a courtroom in Huntsville, Texas. He checked his teeth and straightened his tie with satisfaction. In addition to Kit's bond, his own retainer had just been paid. The publicity that was starting to come his way wasn't bad either. He thought about calling that girl from the university that had turned him down for The Kit Williams Trio concert all those years earlier, but he wasn't sure where she lived anymore. Instead, he called Joel Menken in New York; the creep never even thanked him.

☽

On the night of August 1st, 1972, Kit Williams was completely spent; he watched through the small oval window as the airplane circled under a full and brilliant moon and descended across the familiar, unmistakable lights of Manhattan, making its way to the borough of Queens and LaGuardia airport; and he exhaled a long, hopeful breath of relief. But as the plane wheels touched down, they bounced and skidded a bit before they took hold – not unlike how the irony of his current reality was just now bouncing and skidding into place in his mind: Kit Williams … world-famous folk singer … high school track star … Ruth Williams' beautiful baby boy … had a prison record.

☽

OPEN

PART THREE

Riding to Taos.

August 1 - September 10, 1972

"In Taos with Roddy. Sam's with me. Come if you want. Left money. Call Jimmy re: gig. – Always, Z."

Suzanna's handwriting was as unique and creative as she was; it also leaned backward into her insecurities and held its breath in fear of falling.

Everyone except Kit called her "Zanna." She even referred to herself that way and signed her notes with a simple "Z," following the consistent, single word, "always." "Always what?" Kit often wondered. Always loving? Always perfect? Always angry? Always searching? Always talented beyond belief? Always the love of my life? Always wanting more? Always deserving more? Those last two for sure. Always wanting and deserving so much more than he was capable of giving her, Kit was painfully aware.

As a professional freelance writer, Suzanna was known for her descriptive narrative – creating a sense of place, an experiential sense of being for the reader. Her personal correspondence, on the other hand, was woefully cryptic, as if she'd used up all her words on assignment and sent home the tired left over bits, the dirty laundry that even she didn't want to handle any more than necessary.

Kit left the note where he had found it, tucked into the clay bowl on the small painted table that stood next to the front door of the apartment. It's where they kept their keys and exchanged their notes.

He went into the kitchen, opened the freezer compartment of the refrigerator, and pulled out the pint of mint chocolate chip ice cream he knew would be waiting there for him. Grabbing a spoon from a drawer, he lifted the top off the container and flipped it into the trash. He ate directly from the frosted round cardboard carton as he walked into the bathroom. He stripped off his clothing, dropping it on the floor behind him, turned on the bathtub taps, and slid down into the streaming, steaming water with ice cream still in hand. He adjusted the water faucets with his feet, and finished the melting ice cream, drinking the last bit straight from the soggy carton. He rinsed the spoon in the bathwater, carefully placed it on the bath mat next to the empty, lopsided ice cream container, slid farther down into the water, and thought about going to Taos.

☾

Over the next few days and weeks, Kit went through the motions of life. He bought groceries and ate in coffee shops. He did his laundry and cleaned the bathroom. He walked empty streets on Sunday mornings and rode packed subways on Friday afternoons. He sat in Central Park, read newspapers, worked the crossword puzzles.

He called friends, listened to his mother over the phone, listened to his lawyer across a desk, tried to reach Suzanna, and met regularly with his probation officer. The media had picked up the scent of him being back in New York, and he dodged them the best he could; but his fame had caught fire again – wrapped in his new bad-boy image of Mexican drugs and a Texas trial and Huntsville prison time. He spoke with several club owners about gigs: one no longer wanted him with his new-found reputation; another was drawn to it, wanted to exploit it, wanted to exploit him. In the end, he politely hung up on them all. And he thought about hanging up on his life. But guilt was the stronger emotion. He owed all that bond money to everyone he knew – including his mother. He would, of course, get it back from the court after his trial; but he had no idea when that would happen, and he felt compelled to pay off the obligations as soon as he could. How would he ever repay Suzanna?

At night he slept alone on Suzanna's side of the bed, smelling her pillow. And, too often, he would fall into dreams set in the old apartment in Fort Wayne. He dreamed of the refrigerator in its hideaway alcove. He dreamed of running track, and he could hear his friend Jacob right behind him … and then he couldn't hear him anymore. And he ran until he thought his heart would burst. And he awoke again, to another morning of lost reality.

One morning, about a month after his return to New York, Kit got up and dressed, ate breakfast, washed the dishes. Then he picked up his wallet and keys, locked up the apartment, and walked without purpose for several miles, eventually coming to the edge of an old freight train yard that seemed to be still in service. He sat down among the scrub and rocks, the broken bottles and ragged-edged sections of chainlink fence. He watched the trains for hours – arriving and departing, moving and static. He was particularly intrigued with those cars that were separated from their engines, impotent and useless, yet somehow waiting for life to come find them again, to bring them back to consciousness, to meaningfulness. Even those that were wrapped in dust, profaned with graffiti, and hidden behind rows of sameness, waited with something like anticipation. One of the trains he was watching suddenly started to inch into motion, and he saw a man swinging up into one of its moving boxcars. The figure had some sort of satchel slung over his shoulder and back. And Kit supposed that he could buy one like it at the Army Navy store. Perhaps a canteen as well.

The next few days broke apart into a series of random moments: buying a used canvas backpack, filling it with socks, rolled up underwear, a toothbrush, a razor, deodorant, a clean shirt, an extra pair of jeans, a new sweater he never liked, a book of crossword puzzles, a fountain pen, a pack of five cigars. The satchel seemed full, so he decided he was ready. At the back of a closet shelf, he had found an old sleeping bag he and Suzanna had used in Mexico. It seemed ages since he had laid in it, smelled its mustiness and faint sweetness of weed. And there was a canvas-covered canteen, dented and slightly sour, but still watertight. He hid his cash in his shoes – old hiking boots, stiff from time and disuse; he laced them up tightly, too tightly. The lumps of cash in them were rather uncomfortable, but he practiced walking, then running up and down the back stairs of the apartment building and thought he would get used to it; he felt reassured, somehow, by the discomfort. He thought briefly, too, about his probation. He was not allowed to leave the state without permission. But how do you ask permission for something you couldn't explain? How can you ask permission to run from your life, to run for your life? He thought perhaps they might simply forget about him. And so, he simply forgot about them.

  He was at the rail yard again. It seemed terribly wide and open, yet cluttered and impenetrable. And then he was clamoring into it all. It seemed to breathe out across him – a hard metallic smell of iron and oil and flint, like spent matches and overheated machinery, of things used up and forgotten. The sun kept flashing too brightly in his eyes, but he thought he saw movement in the shadows. And a train was pulling out and he was running toward it. Running for it simply because it was moving – going somewhere – and it would carry him someplace.

  His breathing ached, his lungs were filling with dust and oily, crusty air. His canvas backpack felt stiff and heavy and pulled at his strength, holding him back. He couldn't remember what he had packed in it, what he had felt so important to carry with him. He gripped the bedroll in his right hand. The canteen slipped off his shoulder and banged against his right shin with every step. He tripped perilously a few times. So he tried to watch the wooden cross ties and steel rails beneath his feet, while still focusing on the open freight car door – reaching for it, lunging toward it. Just as his fingers gripped tentatively around the edge of the rattling door, a hand reached out and clenched around his wrist; the hand was dirty and tanned and strong, and it pulled at him. Kit flung his bedroll into the car, his canteen fell onto the tracks behind him. The hand from inside the moving train shifted and grabbed hold of his backpack, half lifting him up and into the dark cavern of the empty boxcar. Kit lay flat on his belly on the dank weather-hardened wood floor; he felt his heart thudding wildly against it, and he recalled a similar strong, sure hand pulling him up from a raging river onto solid but damp land in Texas. This time, the backpack had been dislodged and pressed uncomfortably against his own gritty sweat at the back of his neck. He began to choke and cough. The hand that had yanked him up the last few feet into the moving train thumped him on his back.

"Just stay still for a minute. Your breath will catch up to you," a voice in the dark shouted at him over the din and the metal-on-metal scream of the wheels on the tracks. And gradually, it seemed as if the train was gaining speed in perfect inverse proportion to Kit's heartbeat slowing.

Kit pulled himself to a sitting position, slid his backpack to the floor, and dragged and scooted it farther into the car. His eyes were adjusting to the dark and he saw a man squatting near him. The sun outside was high and brilliant, making the shadows inside deep. But as he became accustomed to the contrast, Kit could make out the features and overall appearance of the man. He had long, light brown hair curling out from under a black knit hat, a slightly rough mustache, dirty worn jeans, a grubby pullover shirt with sleeves pushed up to the elbows, heavy work boots, a genuine smile across good teeth. For some reason, Kit was surprised at how young the man was. Perhaps he expected someone more worn, more ragged, more used up. Perhaps he had not wanted to be in the company of youth.

The other man didn't try to speak. He stood and walked with practiced ease across the madly bouncing, shuddering floor and then leaned against the wall near the edge of the open door, watching the passing view.

Kit's eyes went to the exterior view as well. By then the train was clear of the train yard, but still well within civilization. Junk yards and ancient weary buildings, rusty cars and piles of discarded brick, shacks that leaned and fences that no longer separated anything, all blurred past. A few thin, sickly trees sprouted inexplicably every once in awhile. And birds stuck against the ill-formed branches, braced for the passing wind that was created by the train as it sucked and pushed at their wings. And over the top of all the base, black detritus, the city rose, thrusting its wealth and commerce, its pretense and perceptions, ever higher – as if it were standing on its toes, trying to physically separate itself as far as possible from its lost and forgotten foundation of heaps and pieces.

Kit wondered where the train was going. It seemed as if it was headed west. Perhaps he could ride it all the way to New Mexico. Perhaps he wouldn't want to, he reconsidered, as the car lurched and bounced and twisted like a giant fish trying to purge itself of him. He thought of Jonah, the man who tried to run from God ... and he thought of Pinocchio, the boy who wasn't real and acted mostly on impulse. Kit identified with them both.

The next jolting turn brought his thoughts back to the moment. And his hands clutched at the side of the boxcar as he tried to steady himself, but they scraped along a surface that was rough and ragged and unsure. And so his mind tried to clutch at the past few days and weeks of time, grabbing at their rough-cut images.

☽

Kit and the other man in the boxcar rode in silence for quite a few hours – although their environment was far from silent. The ride was, in fact, excruciatingly loud, so filled with material noise that it precluded any casual conversation. That, and the flailing motion, made sleep out of the question. Twice, the train had slowed but never quite stopped, and the younger man had shouted the explanation to Kit: "Crew change." And then it resumed its previous jarring speed. Eventually, however, the train did twist and angle its way onto a siding; and after a number of final jolts and shakes, and the sound of metal pounding and scraping, it came to a grinding, bone-rattling, halt.

Kit looked out into the setting sun, into seemingly nowhere. His body felt physically beaten, and his ears rang in the sudden quiet.

The other man grinned at him and cautiously held out his hand in greeting. "I'm Wade," he said. His eyes held fast to Kit's face.

"Kit Williams," Kit replied. "Thanks for helping me."

"This is your first ride, isn't it?" Wade observed. "You were lucky I was there to pull you up. You never catch out on the fly like that … unless you're being chased or something. It's a good way to get killed."

Kit nodded his appreciation and understanding.

"Do you mind if I ask where you're headed?" Wade inquired.

"New Mexico, I hope," Kit said almost to himself. "What about you? Where are you going?"

"Wherever this takes me," Wade replied. "And wherever I find the stories." He gave Kit a good long look again. And then, as if making a decision within himself, he walked over to a black-shadowed corner of the boxcar and picked up a leather strap attached to a very professional-looking 35-millimeter camera. Next to it was a heavily taped-together lens case, along with a thickly rolled sleeping bag, a bulging canvas satchel, and a gallon jug of water. "I'm photo documenting the lives of railroad tramps. Following the men. Hearing their stories. Trying to preserve it on film, on paper. They're a dying breed, a fading way of life."

The man was, in fact, a brilliant photographer. Primarily self-taught, but with an eye that can only be born into a soul. His technical skill had been developed through discipline and experimentation, as well as intuition. He studied and experienced, saw and sensed. His work was insightful, compelling, and unaccountably beautiful, haunting in stark black and white. He added to this an ear for cultural language, a mind for remembering conversations, and a heart for finding the dignity and poignancy of a personal history and sense of self. Kit would eventually discover that the man was a gifted teller of stories.

"I've been doing this – catching out on trains and finding tramps and jungles – for about a year now, I guess," Wade responded to Kit's interest. "Maybe it's been longer. It's easy to lose time. I've circled the country at least once anyway."

Wade was a loner – by nature as well as intention. Yet this newcomer awoke a protective impulse within him. Kit obviously had no idea what he was doing, nor how very real the danger could be while doing it. Men riding the rails often partnered up with one another – someone to watch their back, someone with whom to share the emptiness of time and a good story, maybe half a cigarette or a small ration of coffee, along with miles and miles of walking. But even then, they never completely let down their guard. And they accepted that they would not be fully trusted in return.

Kit stood up and looked out the door of the resting boxcar into the bleak surroundings. "So ... do we get off here? Change cars? Or will this one be going again soon?" He had already begun thinking of Wade as a possible traveling companion and guide through this unknown world, hoped he could have his help – possibly all the way to New Mexico. He somehow trusted Wade intuitively and with a strange sense of growing desperation.

"Either way," Wade replied cryptically, his wariness still evident. Even though he had recognized Kit Williams' name and face almost immediately, he had learned to not ask – or answer – too many questions. "This would be a good time to eat," he offered, "maybe get some sleep. Sleeping on a moving train can be challenging, as you may have noticed."

Wade gathered up all his gear, jumped down from the car and started scanning the shadows and outlines of the area with a practiced eye. He was searching for a tramp jungle, a patch where a fire could be built, ideally unseen by any train personnel and other authorities; while some of those folks could be kind and helpful, even friendly, others were openly hostile, and there was no telling which sort he'd run into at any given place or time. He was also carefully discerning if there was a nearby town – if there was any ambient light, and in which direction it might be found.

Kit jumped down after him, but left his heavy backpack and bed roll in the recesses of the empty car. "Will my stuff be okay if I leave it in there for now?" he asked Wade, motioning behind them.

"Might be," Wade answered as he continued to walk away. "Might be safe all the way to the west coast without you – if the car starts to move again and you're not on it."

Kit immediately ran back to the boxcar and removed his belongings.

When he caught up to Wade again, Kit realized the other man had found what he had been looking for. Carved out of the shadows beneath a seemingly disused overpass was a patch of cleared ground. Rocks had been moved to the edges, making it possible to open a bedroll, or pull up a piece of cardboard to sit on; while in the center of the clearing a circle of rocks had been left for a campfire and cooking. Other debris had been pushed aside, too – trash and discards, tin cans and empty bottles, the final scraps of life. But bits of wood and old newspaper had been carefully secured at one edge of the fire circle. Left by previous travelers passing through this place and shared experience.

Kit walked unhesitatingly into the space, and started to examine the surroundings. He thought it odd that the fire circle was so far under the overpass, where the smoke might get trapped. Wade, however, had stopped at the edge of the darkness and was simply peering into its recesses.

From out of the farthest shadow, a coarse voice said without any discernible emotion: "Sometimes it's best ta build yer fire where it caint be seen," seemingly reading Kit's unexpressed thoughts.

Greatly startled, Kit abruptly stopped. But Wade responded to the voice with his own quiet reserve: "Mind if we pull up in here for a bit?" The shadow-voice grunted, and Wade seemed to take it as an assent. He nodded to Kit and piled his own things a few feet farther into the space. Kit simply followed his lead.

As the sun settled down for the evening, the old tramp eventually worked his way out of the shadows and began to build a fire. Wade and Kit contributed additional scavenged bits of wood and paper to it.

The tramp might have been any age, from any place and time, Kit thought. He was dirty and worn, with a stench that wafted toward them whenever the breeze shifted, and he apologized for it. He said he couldn't remember the last bath he had taken. But he had just acquired a bit of soap from a public toilet, so he was sure he'd be able to use it soon. Kit felt moved by the man's embarrassment. His beard was nothing but scruff and dirt. His hair hung long and loose in strings across his face, and it was surprisingly curly; there was no telling its color, or the amount of gray it may have had in it. He wore an old army cap pushed back on his head. His rundown shoes were held together with black electrical tape; he wore no socks. A bandana around his neck served in many capacities, as did his shirt sleeves, which were long and ragged and had not seen buttons in a very long time. His grey pants hung against his too thin frame, cinched in at the waist with a length of scrap leather. Most of his teeth were discolored or missing. And he spoke in a jagged kind of language that seemed to fit with the rest of his brokenness.

As Wade and the tramp each pulled tins of food from their packs, Kit realized with embarrassment that he had not packed anything to eat; he also envisioned his canteen of water bouncing along the ground, abandoned on the tracks many miles back. But Wade took pity on him and shared his meager can of pork and beans, lending him a small bent spoon. The tramp offered him his coffee. And out of desperation and not wanting to offend, Kit drank a bit from the old man's cup, literally shutting his eyes to the sight and smell of the hand that generously passed it to him. Wade looked on and grinned.

After the meal, the three shared cigarettes. Kit was hesitant to take out his small pack of high-end cigars. He continued to watch Wade for his cues in rail-riding etiquette. Nothing in his life experiences – including his recent time spent in Huntsville prison – had prepared him for this.

The eerie, still, darkness was flickered and slivered by small receding flames, and was wrapped in the brown smell of burned beans and tobacco smoke and human sweat, and Kit had the sense that he was somehow simply a spectator to another side of reality – observing, listening. Wade, however, was quietly, subtly, encouraging the third man into conversation. The man's name was – or at least he said it was – Jack.

Jack had pulled another crushed and bent hand-rolled cigarette from his shirt pocket and shoved it into his mouth. He'd picked up a stick from the fire to light it, and his face shown pale against the deep black hollows under his eyes and cheeks in its glow. And then he began relating his stories, his memories, rasping them out as if they were very old, but being told for the first time. Kit and Wade believed most of them, and were touched by all of them in some way or another: Wade because they gave him more depth and texture for his work; Kit with a growing sense of being deeply exposed and unprotected, and feeling as ragged and raw as the cinderblocks against which he was leaning.

In between the stories, all three men sat and smoked in silence. And behind Kit's eyes, his father crept in among them, unwelcome but insistent.

"There was this guy they called Christmas Tree. He got that name 'cause of how he'd go into those Christmas tree lots at night 'n steal Christmas trees 'n take 'em into the taverns aroun' Spookaloo 'n sell 'em. He'd come into a tavern, draggin' a tree b'hin' 'im, 'n go from one end a the bar ta the other, askin' guys if they wanted to buy the tree. 'N when he sold it, he'd go back to the lot 'n git himself another. Then one Christmas he didn't show up 'n ever'body started askin' 'bout 'im 'n wonderin' what happened to 'im. Come to find out, ol' Christmas Tree'd been ridin' through Wenatchee in a boxcar, 'n the door was open only a little bit, a foot er two. He was pokin' his head outta the op'nin', 'n the units jammed on the brakes er an air hose broke er somethin', 'n the train stopped sudden like, 'n the door snapped shut 'n cut off ol' Christmas Tree's head. Ev'ry year, 'roun' Christmas, somebody'll start talkin' 'bout Christmas Tree. They kinda miss 'im in Spookaloo."

"Most times them boxcar doors won't budge; they's always bent 'n shit, but once in a while ye'll git one that'll move on ya if the car gits banged 'roun' good. I rode through a hump once when I was sleepin'. When my car hit bottom I was throwed

forward four, five feet. First off, I thought I was in a wreck. Got up ta look 'roun', 'n it was black as a coal bin in there. The door'd near slammed shut. Only one door'd been open 'n the force a the hump'd near closed it. There was this slit a light comin' in from where the door wasn't quite shut, 'n I went over 'n tried pullin' the door back, but it wouldn't give. Them things weigh better 'n five hunnert pounds. It was only open an inch or two, so I waited there by the op'nin' fer someone to come along. Musta been four, five hours went by b'fore this car knocker come 'roun'. I could hear his footsteps on the gravel outside, 'n when he's passin' right by the door, I give a yell. I sez, 'Hey, git me outta here.' He come over ta the door, 'n he sez, 'You stuck in there?' I sez, 'Sure am.' 'N he sez, 'How long ya been in there?' He was kind of a young fella, so I thought I'd shit 'im a little. I sez, 'Three weeks, 'n I'm jus' now beginnin' ta smell bad. Nah,' I sez. 'Only been in here a few hours, but I'd like ta git the hell out b'fore this here train pulls out.' 'N me 'n him both tried to pull on the door; him from outside 'n me from the inside, 'n it still wouldn't give. He went 'n got a few other guys, 'n they wedged some two by fours in the op'nin' 'n pried it jus' enough so's I could squeeze out. Took 'bout an hour ta git me outta there. It's the only time in twenty-five years I had a door close on me. Most times them things ain't gonna move."

> "I been carryin' the stick for twenty-five years now. I ain't got an education. I got a background."

"When I'm pullin' into a town at night, I watch out to see 'at no on sees me git off the train. I look fer a place to sleep, all the time makin' sure no one's got their eye on me. Best to pick a spot where there's a little cover, in some weeds er bushes. You gotta watch yerself 'roun' the yards at night. In some towns, a tramp wouldn' dare go to sleep, 'cause chances are he wouldn' be wakin' up; place crawlin' with jackrollers. Now there's some towns where I'll right away build me a fire in the yards but sit with my back to some'um. Stay up all night. I've stayed awake a few days straight in towns 'at's bad, waitin' on the next train out. Sometimes you don' even wanna build a fire; 'tract too much attention. ... If there's a jungle fire goin', stay away. You don' wanna walk in on a camp in the dark. Wait till mornin' if you feel like bein' socialable.... There's jungles 'at e'en bulls wouldn' be caught settin' foot in at night. They might come to the edge a the tracks an' shine their light aroun', but they ain't gonna go pokin' their nose 'roun' in the dark. 'Fraid they'll git knocked on the head er some'um.
... That son of a bitch over in Lakeland seen me hop off a westboun' one time. I knowed he seen me. Had his flashlight right square on me when I hopped off. I ducked in the trees an' kept an eye out fer him. Pitch dark down there. He walked to the edge 'n shined the light all aroun'. Can't see nothin' lookin' in a woods

like you can seein' out. Didn't stay more 'n half a minute 'fore he went off. Watched him from the trees."

"Got hold of a jug one night 'n caught out on that Stockton line. I was by myself, 'n it ain't good ta be drinkin' alone 'cause ya wind up drinkin' too much. If yas got a guy ta split with, why ya only drink half as much, 'n ya stretch the drinkin' out 'cause yer talkin' while yer drinkin'. Ya don't git too drunked up that way. Well, I drunk that jug pretty quick 'n passed out. I dunno what I was doin'. I musta still been half drunk, 'n thought the train'd stopped in Stockton. I got up, went over ta the door, 'n bailed out, 'n goddamn if that train weren't still movin'. Shit, hittin' that track ballast at twenty mile an hour'll sober ya up mighty quick."

"One thing 'bout tracks, they only goes two ways: where you been and where you goin.' Damn difficult to get lost that-a-way."

It would be decades before Kit would come across an exhibition of Wade's work from that time; it was called "Following the Tracks," and it was presented under the name of "D. Wade Wilder," causing Kit to wonder at the fact that he had never known Wade's full name or what the "D" stood for. The exhibit featured years worth of remarkable black and white photographs, along with the soul-searing stories told by the tramps themselves. And Kit would remember vividly how he had witnessed the hard truth of it firsthand.

Most especially, he would remember that first night – on the edge of the rails, in the shadows of life – and he marveled at Wade's ability to capture it all with such authenticity, such beautiful, terrible honesty.

    Jack and Wade were soon sleeping in fits and starts curled up on their bedrolls, and the fire died grey and cold and wind blown. But Kit sat pressed against a cement piling, grittily awake and aware and bitter with his thoughts, until the dawn birds broke into his unaccustomed vulnerability that verged on fear, as he watched the moon riding away, low in the sky.

☾

Following a meager morning meal of shared tinned stew and weak coffee, Jack caught out on an eastbound train. Kit had given him a pair of his socks, and Jack, too grateful for words, had left him with two hand-rolled cigarettes and the grime from a boney yet sincere handshake.

Wade had suggested a walk into the nearest town for Kit to get some supplies, and had further offered to go with him. They thought perhaps they could both wash up a bit as well. The town was only about three or four miles to the west, but it was not easy going, especially carrying their gear. The way was littered with rocks and trash and scrub. And the early-September temperature was rising with the sun.

To ease the journey, Wade entertained Kit with some stories of his own – experiences he had known while he'd been riding the rails. He talked about the men who were called "streamliners" – those who traveled the tracks without any gear or provisions at all – except for what they wore on their backs or had stuffed in their pockets.

"Streamliners aren't trusted by most of the tramps," he told him. "It's assumed they'll steal from anyone they meet. And tramps have very long memories. I've seen one man catch up with someone who stole a bedroll from him years earlier – and beat the living crap out of him."

Kit suddenly thought of Marcus, the "romancer of women" and the beating he had gotten his first night in Huntsville for having "stolen" another man's woman. "I witnessed something similar not long ago in Huntsville."

"Huntsville, Alabama? Tennessee? Arkansas?" Wade questioned casually.

"Huntsville ... Prison ... Texas," Kit clarified.

"Huntsville Prison ... " Wade left it hanging there, expectant, inviting more.

"Long story."

"Nothing but time."

"I spent two weeks in Huntsville about a month ago. Transporting weed from Mexico. Bonded out. But it's a pretty weak case. I'm trying to kind of sort things through right now. Suzanna – my girlfriend – is in Taos, and I thought I'd try to meet up with her there."

"And your best option was riding the rails?"

"Seemed like a good idea watching someone else do it."

"As it often does," Wade nodded. "Look, I know who you are, I'm a great admirer of your music. Your manager actually bought some of my songs awhile back."

"You're a songwriter?"

"Sometimes. One entire summer I traveled all across Canada – living out of my car with nothing but a girl and a guitar. Some great songs came out of that time, great memories. Lost the girl, though. She disappeared somewhere near New York."

"As they often do. What were some of your songs? Did I record any of them – or The Trio?"

"No. I'm one of the vast number of songwriters that seems destined to remain in obscurity ... a writer of songs sung mostly by friends, and then only when nobody is actually listening."

Wade began mentioning some of the titles of his songs and singing a few bars of them. And Kit was enjoying the experience. And then Wade began talking about how he'd brought a guitar with him on his first rail ride, and how it had been a disaster. The first hard hit between cars and the guitar was severely damaged. It had also proved woefully difficult to carry, and so it was traded along the way for a drinking cup and three potatoes.

By then they had reached the town. And Wade warned Kit that they would be recognized as tramps and avoided as such.

"But I have money," Kit said. "Cash." He had unpacked one of his shoes earlier and shifted some of it to a more accessible pocket.

"It won't matter. I mean, that's good, that will get you what you need and all – but people will still watch your every move, sometimes cross the street to avoid you, may deny you service. We're right up there with homeless and drunks and users when it comes to perception and acceptance and treatment. We all get lumped together. I find it all rather insightful. I once read something a guy wrote about tramps that said they were – let me see if I can remember this all – 'lazy, shiftless, swaggering' (loved that one: swaggering), 'ill-conditioned, irreclaimable, incorrigible, and cowardly' … there was one more, oh yes, 'savage'. Ha. Cowardly *and* savage."

Just on the outskirts of town, they came to a Piggly Wiggly food market. Wade offered to stay outside with the gear while Kit shopped alone and wouldn't attract as much attention.

Stepping into the small store, Kit appreciated its cooled air immediately. The aisles were narrow but well stocked. He thought through his purchases based on Wade's advice – not too heavy, but filling … or reusable.

In the end, he had one large brown paper sack carrying two potatoes, two apples (he'd put back a third for weight), an orange, two cans of pork and beans (one to repay Wade), two cans of soup, a hard roll, a small jar of peanut butter, a small jar of instant coffee, two packages of beef jerky, a half gallon of water, a small pack of "moist towelettes," and two candy bars (one Three Musketeers and one Snickers). He was particularly excited to find a combination can opener and knife, as well as a small aluminum pot, at the end of an aisle near the checkout counter.

As he paid for the items, he took note of the looks he got from the other customers as well as the checkout girl. He thought he probably smelled. He knew he was grubby. But instead of being ashamed, he felt rather giddily proud.

Pocketing his change, he stepped back into the sun and heat, and thought he ought to eat his candy bar on the walk back before it melted, and then he thought that perhaps he should allow Wade to choose his preference first. But Wade was not there. Wade was gone.

Kit had searched under all the eaves and around all the corners of the store, scanned the parking lot, the racks of shopping carts, between parked cars. He'd walked quickly to the road and looked as far as he could in either direction. But Wade was simply gone – along with all of Kit's gear and confidence. For a moment Kit thought he was going to be sick. The parking lot felt like it was moving underneath him, and he widened his stance so he wouldn't fall down. He gripped the grocery bag tighter and felt the sweat on his hands soaking into it, making it slippery, releasing a wet brown paper smell, like a kindergarten project. He wondered if that's how humiliation ought to smell. He reminded himself that he'd only known Wade for about twenty-four hours. But he'd trusted him. He'd been betrayed by him. And it broke his heart. It broke his spirit.

As far back as he would allow himself to remember, Kit had always been the one who did the leaving, the walking away. From The Trio. From his manager. From sports. From his Dad. The only one he'd never left was his mother. And Suzanna. He couldn't imagine ever leaving Suzanna. He needed to call her. He needed to call his mother. He saw a phone booth across the parking lot, started walking toward it, running toward it. Angry and suddenly very tired. So angry. So tired.

The paper grocery bag started to rip, and he clutched it tighter in his arms. He reached the phone booth and set the bag down by his feet. Feeling in his jeans pocket, he found a dime and dropped it into the phone and dialed zero. When the operator came on, he asked to place a collect call and gave his name and his mother's phone number. While the phone rang in his mother's same old apartment in Fort Wayne that they'd shared all those years, his mind crawled back behind the refrigerator. He was there with no reason he could think of or understand. His mother had just gotten home from work but he didn't come out. She was calling his name over and over, and she had started to sound afraid. And he knew he could make her worry with his silence, or put her mind at ease simply by calling back to her. But he just kept listening to her call out for him. Over and over. Out the window. Down the stairwell. Knocking on Rene's door. More and more frightened. More and more sure he was gone. And then he did answer her, and he came out from hiding, and acted as if he hadn't heard her. She was shaking as she held him close to her. He could hear her heart beating. She scolded him, of course, but there was no anger in it. Only fear. And he wondered at how much he had liked that control.

"Hello? Kit, is that you? Are you there?" His mother was calling to him on the phone line. She always spoke too loudly on long distance calls.

"Yeah – hi, Mom – yes, it's me. I'm on the road to Taos to meet up with Suzanna. Just wanted to check in with you. Let you know. You okay?" He made sure his voice was casual and relaxed. His mother could always tell.

"Yes, I'm fine. It's raining here. Starting to feel like fall already. And I haven't even finished the tomatoes from the garden out back. Hope that doesn't mean a long winter." His mother always had to discuss the weather before anything else. It was as if she had to give her mind time to get discussion points in order.

"Wish I were there to have one of your tomato sandwiches," Kit said with complete honesty.

"Are you working?"

"A few gigs here and there," he lied. "I'll be able to repay you – and everyone – soon, really soon."

"That's not why I asked."

"I know."

"Is Suzanna well?"

"Yes – she's good. She's working. Got a feature or something going in New Mexico. That's why she's there." Lies again. Or maybe not. He didn't really know. "I just wanted to check in with you. Let you know where we are. I'll call you again and give you a phone number when I get there."

"Are you driving?"

"I've got to go now, Mom. We'll talk again soon."

"Be careful. I love you."

"Love you, too. Bye."

Kit hung up the receiver and rested his head against it. He wondered if he could call Suzanna, and fished the dime back out of the return slot. He even, for one moment, thought that he might call his probation officer; but he couldn't quite remember his name right then, or his number. It was stifling in the phone booth, and he kicked the door open for air. He had to think. Why had Wade left him? Stolen from him and left him behind like his broken guitar? At least Wade had gotten a few potatoes in trade for the guitar. Of course, he'd gotten some clean underwear and an extra bedroll in trade for Kit. Perhaps Wade was going to turn him in for some kind of reward money. Was there reward money? Kit crouched down and started searching in the torn paper bag for one of the candy bars.

"Hey! There you are. I got us some coffee – some real coffee at that little luncheonette down the street. They won't let us eat inside, but they put some coffee in a couple of takeout cups for us – clean cups. I didn't know what you liked in yours so I left it black." Wade was struggling a bit with all the gear and the two cups of hot coffee, trying to hand one to Kit.

"And I got us a couple of candy bars," Kit replied, reaching them out to Wade without really looking up at him. "Take your pick."

The two men spent what was left of the day using a local laundromat – and washing themselves up as best they could in its restroom. They repacked Kit's new provisions, and then returned to the accommodating luncheonette for several takeout cheese sandwiches wrapped in waxed paper.

Wade had created a sort of waistband carryall for Kit by tying two of his extra socks to his belt, toe to ankle, one on either side of him. Kit had filled the socks with the apples, the orange, the potatoes and the roll. The rest of the food was either fitted into his back pack or rolled into his sleeping bag. With the weight thus evenly distributed, he discovered he was able to carry it and the water jug relatively easily.

According to some town signage, they knew they were somewhere in Pennsylvania. Most of the tracks from there would point them toward Ohio and then Chicago, Wade surmised. So, as the sun started moving closer to the horizon, they made their way back to the rails, and started walking them in search of a jungle where they could wait to catch-out on another train.

As they walked, Kit was aware that Wade had not yet said if he was going to travel with him or not, even on the next leg of the journey. And he was trying to think how he could ask. But before he could speak, Wade said: "You do realize, most tramps aren't going anywhere in particular. They're just riding. They're never arriving … always leaving. Nobody's waiting for them. They have no schedule to keep. That's usually the whole point of doing this."

Kit shifted his gear a bit and then slowed his pace. "I know *you've* got a purpose in doing this." He was finding it hard to breathe and had nearly stopped walking altogether. "And I know you've probably got someone who is waiting for you."

Wade didn't answer, but also didn't stop moving. So Kit willed himself to increase his stride again to catch up, physically and conversationally. "What would you think about coming to Taos with me? I could buy most of the food, if you'd show me how to get there – and watch my back."

It was becoming evident to Kit that he had never felt so broken and unsure in his life as he did at that moment and place in time; although perhaps this odd sense of diffidence had been there all along, stalking him, growing in him over time. It utterly confused him, unnerved him. Once, with a severe case of the flu, he had experienced vertigo, and he thought perhaps it was happening again. Except this was a sort of vertigo of the self: an off-centered, tilt-a-whirl within his sense of being. His mind rewound through all the times he had been alone out on rutted, lawless backroads in Mexico; and to running his heart out on a track without Jacob behind him; and to being in the middle of hundreds of pitch black stages, performing for thousands of faceless strangers, and sleeping in oddly familiar hotels with stiff-sheeted beds, eating their oddly familiar food off of hard plastic trays. He felt again the damp, bleached-cold cell of a state penitentiary in Texas; and he felt the hard splintered back steps of an old two-story house converted into apartments in the left-behind part of Fort Wayne, Indiana. And through it all, he couldn't remember this overwhelming sense of literal disintegration – a feeling that his very soul was separating from his body, shattering into fragments of himself. There had been a time when he had existed safely as two boys, and he could be either of them as needed, as wanted. But this was different and disconcerting, out of reach, out of control. This was like being able to feel the presence of all the selves inside one skin. And yet, he thought that if he looked into a mirror, there might be no image at all.

Wade had remained silent, walking, watching the disappearing sun. Kit tried to clear his voice and his mind and continue the conversation where he'd left off: "You could meet Suzanna. She's a writer. Very talented." But then he finally went silent, too.

Wade stopped walking and pointed toward a small wooded area farther down the rails, not much more than a simple stand of trees, just to the south of the tracks. By looking very closely, they could see a slim ribbon of smoke rising a few yards into it. They started walking toward it.

As they were approaching the edge of the encampment, Wade halted. Looking sideways at Kit, he put his hand on the other man's shoulder and said: "What the hell, why not. I've always wanted to see Taos. I hear they've got these wild mustangs that I'd love to photograph. But let's just get to Chicago first. That's going to be at least another three days or so. And then, my friend, let's seriously think about a couple of bus tickets to New Mexico."

Kit laughed but didn't recognize his own voice. At least he was able to breathe again, and swallow. And, for the moment, the ground beneath him became steadier.

☾

There were two tramps already settled in the jungle. Kit stood back and let Wade do the talking. "Would you mind a couple of strangers joining you?" Wade asked respectfully, and he looked hard at the two men and their gear without appearing to be doing so.

The man on the left turned to his comrade; they both nodded agreement, so Wade stepped into the space.

"Hi. This is Kit ... I'm Wade," he stated simply, as he eased himself to the ground. Kit became aware that no one used their last names in this culture. Perhaps it was a lack of trust. Or perhaps it was a lack of identity. Kit found he related to both.

"Which way's ya' headin'?" the man on the left asked.

"West," Wade replied for them both.

"We is too," the man said. "M' name's John. You kin call him Willie," he jerked his head toward the other man, who simply nodded at them again.

The man called John then pointed toward a section of train that was very near to them, and said, "I think that'n's goin' westward in the morning. Mebbe Indy. I've been askin' 'round, checkin' loads. Think that's a pretty good bet. Yep. Pretty good bet, that one."

Wade turned to Kit with just a look on his face that managed to communicate: *let's catch that one out – better than Chicago, farther South*. And he said, "Thanks, John."

The two men sitting opposite them in the light of the small fire seemed to Kit less tired and scabbed than Jack had the night before. Their clothes were less tattered, their smell less rank. Their faces were even less hollow and lined. They were less vulnerable. Perhaps it was because they had each other. Or maybe they had spent less time on the rails or had families back home somewhere – with some kind of memories to sustain them. Kit never gave a thought as to how he must appear to them. He wouldn't have been able to say how he appeared even to Wade. Right then, he was barely visible to himself.

Dinner that night for Wade and Kit was the rest of the cheese sandwiches, a half an orange each, and some strong instant coffee. Something that was dark and thick and smelled surprisingly good came out of a can that John and Willie heated over the fire and shared. When Kit was pulling apart the orange to split between Wade and himself, he separated a few sections off of his half and offered them to John and Willie as well. They were accepted with obvious, yet unspoken, gratitude.

The night around them had become thick with blue shadows and unnatural breezes, and the sounds of scavengers and lost things. There were scurrying movements and distant dogs barking, the shouts of faraway humans using indistinguishable words. It sounded like neither the city nor the country to Kit. It sounded like a long way from home.

And, then, into this background of sounds and moans, Kit began to add his own voice. He suddenly, unexpectedly, began to sing.

It was a song that had been playing in the very back of his mind, just beneath his consciousness, throughout most of the day. He had recorded it a few years earlier – in the mid-1960s, he thought – and he used it frequently in his live stage shows. It was was about working in the coal mines. The tune itself was a deeply moving lament; the words were a dark anthem to hopelessness and despair. Kit filled it with a haunting beauty. It was as if it recognized and named the loneliness within each of the men seated around the feeble fire that night, himself included. And it gave value to their pain.

There was silence when the song ended, until Willie spoke for the first time, and said simply, "Thanks."

"I ain't heard singin' like that since … a long time ago," John added.

Wade smiled widely at Kit, but didn't tell the other men who his friend was. It was an audience of only three – an audience of tramps, loners, rail-riders – two of whom probably hadn't heard a record or a radio or seen a television in more than a decade, so they would most likely not have even known Kit Williams' name or his music anyway. And, after all, it was Kit's story to tell, if he chose to do so, Wade seemed to sense.

"How 'bout singin' another 'n?" Willie said. "That was real nice."

And so Kit did. And then he sang more. And each song seemed to lay itself down right at their feet with a sort of bitter sweetness that somehow broke open the sense of solitary existence that encased each of them. And it let their own private moments of some remembered beauty and forgotten hope come sliding back into the cracks.

Kit's voice could do that to an audience – whether it was thousands of students crushed into an Ivy League university auditorium, or a handful of sophisticates in a small infamous club. But never had his talent delivered such purpose and message than it did that night, to these few men who were so unknowingly desperate for its empathy and grace.

Somewhere in the middle of the second song, Kit became aware that Wade was taking photographs of them all. It didn't bother him or the other men, so they continued to share the moment with their unique abilities and growing camaraderie.

Afterward, just as all four men were settling into sleep, Wade spoke quietly to Kit: "I hope you're okay with my shooting you tonight. I usually ask first. It was just such perfect light – fire on your face, scattered town light behind you, the shadows. And the other men's profiles were incredible. I appreciate it. I just didn't want to interrupt the music."

"I really barely noticed your shooting. Can I see the photos when they're developed? Who knows, maybe you just shot my next album cover."

"Sure. I'd like to share all of this work publically someday. Not sure who will want to see it. And, by the way," Wade said as he flopped out flat on this bed roll, "I'd love to shoot that album cover. Can't wait for your next release."

But all Kit could do was nod into the darkness. He stretched out on his own bedding and turned his face away from Wade, away from the other men, away from the light. He tried to let nothing into his head except the words of a song. Just words of a song. That night, Kit slept without dreaming.

🌙

Kit awoke to that liminal time when just before sunrise and just after sunset seem to be identical – with only the coolness of a breeze to declare the coming of dawn. He watched its rising beauty, floating for a moment in a safe, soft, place of not knowing.

Then, breaking into the liminality, there was an alarming sound of loud banging – hard wood on metal, drawing near, like steel drums on a death march, marching ever closer.

Wade was also kicking on the soles of Kit's feet with his own boot as he was hastily rolling up his bedding. The other men were rushing to gather themselves and their gear together as well.

"Bulls," Wade stated flatly. "Railroad patrolmen. And by the way they're banging on the cars with their sticks, they're not in the mood for us."

Kit swept together his things in a sort of stupor; rolled it up, stuffed it in, tucked it under his arms. And, for some reason, he blurted out, "What about breakfast?" But he quickly realized he was talking to the backs of three swiftly departing men.

"Seriously … ?" Wade called over his shoulder. "Come on! Just come on! Get your ass into that boxcar now!"

The train had started to move and John was first up. He reached out a hand to Willie, then to Kit. Wade threw his gear in to Kit and swung himself up, grasping John's outstretched hand. The railroad men gave the car a final hit with their clubs – but it was more of a sendoff than a threat.

The car was, indeed, headed west, Kit realized with relief after catching his breath and bearings. He stared out the open door for awhile at the sun rising, and then he leaned in Wade's direction and shouted: "So ... that's a 'no' on breakfast?" Wade's laugh was lost to the noise of the ride.

It would take them three more days of hard travel to make it through Indiana. John and Willie had split away from them by then, headed toward Chicago. But on the west-central edge of the state, just inside the border from Illinois, the train stopped in a small, fading farm town, and they were able to once again restock their food supplies.

They purchased a variety of packaged foods at a local family grocery store, and cleaned up at the corner Clark gas station. And with Wade employing all the charm he had at his calling, they were permitted to patronize a small storefront diner for a hot, home-style meal – as long as they sat in the end booth and stowed their gear out of sight under their seats.

In the wide front window of the diner, a blue neon sign glowed "Evie's." And from the warm steam-filled kitchen, the Blue Plate Special featured some of the finest meatloaf and mashed potatoes Kit could ever remember tasting. The meatloaf itself was thick with sweet onions and oozed tomato sauce and was heavy on his fork. The potatoes were yellow with butter and just lumpy enough so he knew they were the real thing. There were boiled green beans, limp in a small dish on the side, chunked with bacon and plenty of salt and pepper. And there were orange jello cubes that slid down his throat between bites. The coffee was hot and strong and fresher than he expected, the cream clouded it like a sky rolling in a storm. And the waitress called them both "Sir" and brought them extra warm, soft, dinner rolls, with little pats of butter on small cardboard squares that were half melted and slipped off their knives.

Their seats were high-backed red plastic benches, their table was chrome-edged with a formica top and chipped corners, but wonderfully clean. Overhead fluorescent lights hummed and blinked. While a very large orange cat sat blinking from a window ledge across the room, half hidden behind a potted pothos plant. The linoleum covered floor had been over-scrubbed for years and was patched here and there with mismatched tiles. Seated at the counter, there was a gathering of regulars discussing the merits of new trucks and old dogs and the construction of an appliance production plant coming soon to the edge of town.

Neither Kit nor Wade wasted time talking.

After they had both pushed back their plates, and their waitress (whose name they learned was Kay, and who was the daughter of Evie herself) had brought them scoops of ice cream in glass footed bowls, they began to discuss the rest of the trip to Taos.

In the end, they did catch out on freight trains all the way to New Mexico, even though that meant almost a week more of rough, unpredictable travel. But they stepped off their last boxcar in Santa Fe, and took an ancient, groaning, public bus the final seventy miles north into Taos itself.

🌙

Along the way, Kit had grown vaguely attached to this jagged way of living: to being hungry most of the time; to going sometimes a couple of days without sleep; to meeting thickly scarred men with first names only and ingrained watchfulness; to being stared at and stared down; and to feeling lost and to feeling saved and to wondering at the thin fragile thread that separated them and wove them all together. And he had grown in appreciation for Wade's work and his sense of respect for the men he was photographing, the life he was documenting, the culture he was preserving.

They had shared the remaining miles with half-a-dozen tramps. There was Joe from Kentucky, who had a wife and family back home, but who just couldn't seem to stay put for more than a couple of months at a time; he worried that his oldest son was going to follow in his footsteps. And there was Al from somewhere in the midwest that he never specified and who carried a large handgun and showed it somewhat surreptitiously to everyone and made Kit extremely uncomfortable. There was another Joe, partnered up with a man named Frank, both from Michigan, both full of bad jokes and fantastic stories about different folks they'd met and fights they'd won and ways they'd outsmarted the Bulls. They said they buried supplies all along their routes so they could always have a bit of something they might need without carrying it all with them (although they were rather reticent about saying how they knew where to find it again). And there was Charlie, who seemed remarkably educated, intelligent, and in terrible pain – both physical and emotional; he'd been wounded in Vietnam, and just never made it home again. Wade took their photographs. And Kit sang them songs.

Between rides, Kit and Wade found they could communicate well about music. They talked about Wade composing new songs for Kit when they got to New Mexico. They also talked – often with great humor, often with great regret – about their lives, especially their childhoods.

They were getting closer to the southwest and the New Mexico desert, and the nights were becoming noticeably colder, more brilliant with stars and an expanse of being. One such night, when it was very late and still, Wade told Kit that his dad had died when he was twelve. Kit confided in return about his own wretched and aching relationship with his father and how he had virtually lost him to his drinking when he was just nine; about the holes it had torn in him, the sense that he was missing entire pieces of himself because of it. And how he could never quite understand why, or stop believing that he might have done something to keep him from leaving. He shared the grief and guilt of it, and was glad for the fact that darkness and night surrounded them.

After awhile, Kit asked Wade how he had lost his father, but Wade turned away into the long, black silence. And Kit had the terrible understanding that some stories needed to be left alone, some pain left untouched.

☽

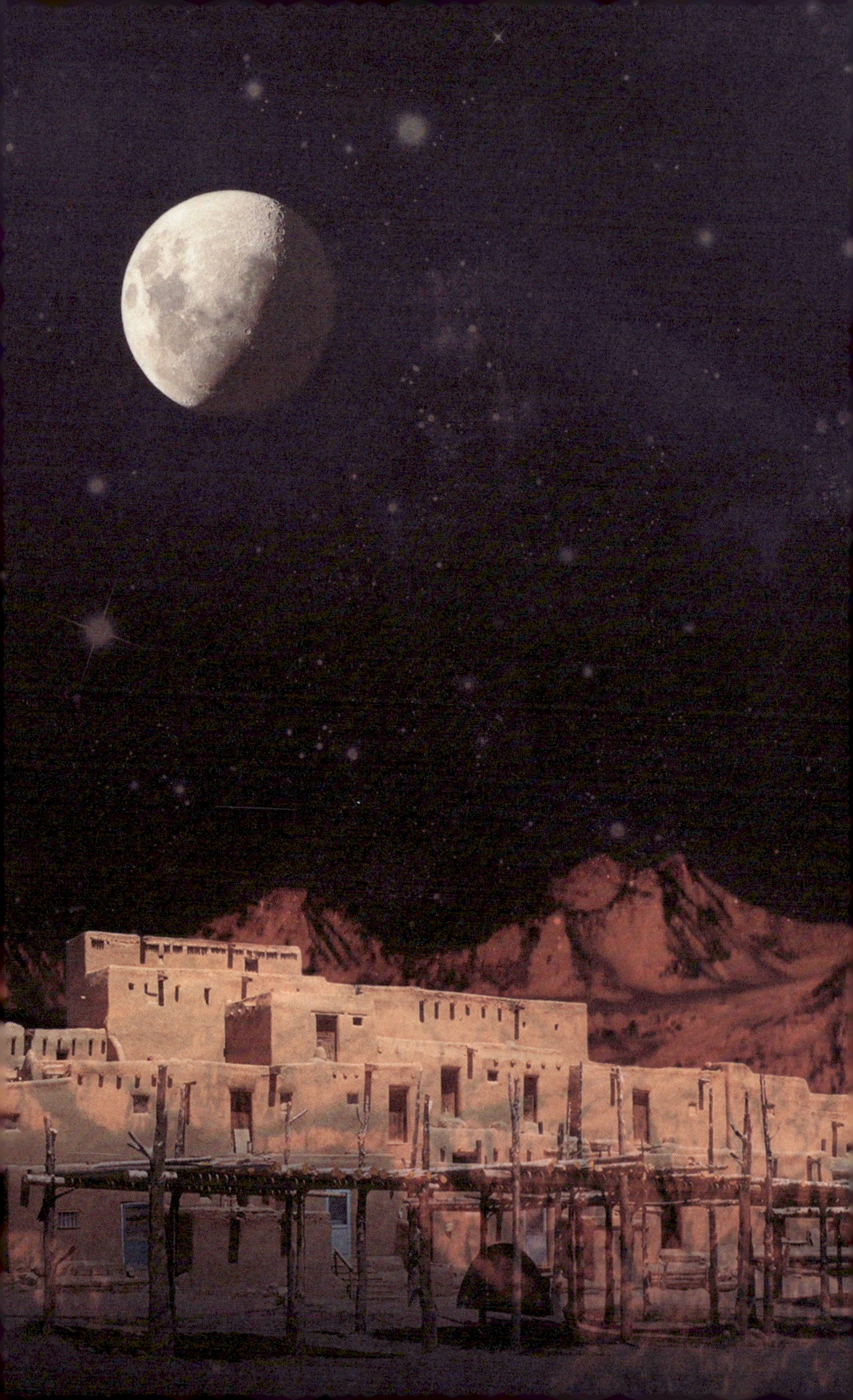

PART FOUR

Taos, New Mexico.

September 10 - October 1, 1972

On Sunday, September 10, at 8:22 a.m., the bus from Santa Fe, New Mexico, arrived in Taos and deposited two very grungy, extremely weary, yet highly anticipatory strangers into its existence. No one took the least bit of notice.

    The centuries-old plaza that formed the center of Taos was quiet, at peace with itself, as it gently welcomed the newcomers along with the sun that was already warming its cobblestones, its thin pale dirt, its crumbling adobe buildings.

    A small number of native residents sat or stood in tight-faced groups and randomness along the stone ledges that were once the walls of the original plaza buildings, but which now simply defined its edges and place in history. A few people were wandering along the plaza storefronts, wiping at the window dust with their hands, pressing their faces close to see nothing new beyond the shadows of the shuttered-up Sunday.

    The buildings of the plaza were almost all crafted of adobe in the distinct and traditional style that had long ago intermarried indigenous Indian, Spanish, and Mexican architecture, building materials, and techniques. But here and there, a few insignificant wooden structures inserted themselves, blending in as best they could. To the west was a lovely old classic adobe Catholic church. And sauntering off in every other direction there were scatterings of homes and studios and unassuming dwellings that once and again sheltered writers and artists, musicians and historic personalities, as well as the natives.

    Wade was drawn to an open vegetable stand that had been set up in front of one of the closed stores, attended by some of the newer "natives" – members of the ever-evolving, ever-earnest hippie culture that had begun to seek out Taos as a place to live a more authentic, clean, unspoiled life. There were two women – caucasian, but brown from the sun, with long hair done up in braids. One wore her plaits wrapped around her head; the other had pulled hers back with a faded blue bandana. The first woman had on a pair of old bib-overalls that seemed too large for her, rolled up at the legs, with a much mended and worn soft t-shirt beneath it. Her feet were bare. The other had on a multicolored skirt that skimmed her legs just above the sandals on her feet. A bright pink shirt thinly covered her bare breasts. A man was with them: African-American, dressed in loose, low-slung pants and no shirt, his naturally brown skin smooth and tinted red by the morning sun. He had a beaded band around his head and sandals on his feet and he carried across his back a very young child – not much more than a baby really – in a sort of homemade sling of a lovely tie-died material. The child was sleeping soundly and looked half Black, half White, and full of health and contentment. She was one of the most beautiful babies Wade could ever remember seeing.

    As Wade drifted toward the welcoming greeting of the vegetable sellers, Kit began to look for a phone booth; he grasped in his right hand a scrap of paper with the local number Suzanna had given him. She was staying with Roddy, a friend of hers from college who owned a sort of rambling guesthouse/compound – a main house surrounded by a gathering of small single- and two-room dwellings just outside of town. Here, she rented out rooms and fed guests and took in stray dogs and cats and artists and writers in no particular order. Roddy was a talented artist herself; but she had spent most of her time over the past several years actively involved with the local alternative newspaper, until it had finally struggled to a close the year before. But the room rents she collected kept food on the table – for herself and everyone else who pulled up a chair around it. And now she spent as much time as she could rediscovering her own art.

A few minutes later, Kit came up to Wade slowly dragging his bedroll in the dust behind him. He watched as Wade paid for and consumed a huge whole tomato, the juice and seeds running down his beard stubble and onto his shirt front. He quickly bent over, dodging the onslaught of sweet tomato juices and laughed, and then looked up sideways at Kit.

"What's wrong?" Wade asked.

"She's gone."

"Who's gone – Suzanna? What do you mean?"

"She's gone," Kit stated flatly again, without inflection or belief. "Roddy says she didn't think I was coming. She hadn't heard from me in such a long while. She's gone to Aspen. She's gone to do a piece on a concert up there. She's not here." He turned to Wade, looking him square in the face. But there was nothing there for Wade to read.

"I'm sorry," was all Wade could think to say. "What do you want to do?"

"Take a bath. I want to take a bath … a real bath … eat some real food … sleep in a real bed," Kit said simply.

"At Roddy's?"

"It's this way." And Kit began walking north, still dragging his gear and regret behind him.

As they walked, Kit looked straight into the Sangre de Cristo Mountains that bent and folded and raised up their backs across the north and eastern horizons. The blood of Christ, they were called – perhaps in recognition of the haunting blood-red color that drenched their shoulders when the desert sun was setting; yet certainly in remembrance of the last words of a long-ago Spanish priest as he lay bleeding, dying, killed by the natives in retaliation for all he had murdered in them in his innocent egoism. Kit had always sympathized with the Indians, but wondered if the subsequent name given to the mountain range was actually a sly expression of eternal accusation and grudge.

He walked and watched the nearest peak. Walked and watched it move away from him with every step he took toward it. His mind told him he was moving nearer, and yet the mountain kept its distance. Always the same distance. And he felt the irony. And he softly chanted it: "It's right there. Right in front of me. I could touch it. But it keeps moving. Keeps leaving. A trick of perspective ... a trick of the mind ... a trick of the Spanish priest ..." And his voice wandered off into the desert shadows along with his thoughts. Wade heard and kept it to himself with sympathetic understanding.

About a mile or so north, they came to a small and unique group of houses – one main house and half-a-dozen smaller buildings skirting around it. And encircling them all was a weather-worn wooden plank fence-line that seemed to serve no purpose, with huge gaps in it at irregular intervals.

The main house was somewhat at the center and very much at the forefront of all the other, smaller dwellings – a mother creature watching over her young.

The smaller buildings were all adobe and hut-like, but the main house was multi-storied, multi-winged; although it, too, was made mostly of adobe with some stone sections and walls.

In the yard, there were thin trees of some kind making thin shade, and bright flowers everywhere, at every doorstep, bursting from strange containers, lining the walkways. The entire property was boldly and unabashedly odd, quirky, free-spirited, a collection built out of time and happenstance and imagination.

Kit carefully opened and walked through the front gate (although the fencing on either side of it was missing entirely). Wade followed him up a flagstone walkway leading to the wide stone steps of a deep front porch. The porch was covered with a wooden arbor, functioning as a portico, draped in flowering bougainvillea and laced with a string of small lights. Both the men stopped to look into the face of the earth-toned house; someone was repainting the trim and shutters a bright blue, but had quit abruptly, leaving the impression of an elderly but still charming grand lady putting on her makeup, interrupted, startled, forgetful, eccentric.

"This is Roddy's," Kit announced rather unnecessarily. The door was standing open, and the smell and sounds of breakfast and hospitality were rolling out on top of a woman's deep and throaty laugh. Kit dropped his gear where he stood; Wade picked it up, and piled it with his own to one side of the porch steps. *Best not to bring it inside,* he decided. He nodded to a couple who was sitting, eating rolled-up pancakes with their fingers, at the far end of the porch; they nodded back, but Kit didn't notice them.

"Roddy!" Kit called out as they stepped through the open doorway. "It's me, Kit, and my friend Wade."

They had entered the dark, cool, tiled entryway, and were passed by a young girl who was leaving with an empty woven fruit basket under her arm: "Hola," she said shyly.

"Hola, cómo estás," Kit replied automatically.

"Hi," Wade added.

Off to the right, Kit led them through a large dining room with a beamed ceiling. A long farm table ran down the middle of the room, with a handful of mismatched people sitting in equally mismatched chairs on both sides of the table, their backs turned to two wooden sideboards on opposite walls. At the front end of the room, a wide hinged window – almost as tall as the room itself – was opened to the fresh air, casually propped open by an old-world-style candlestick that must have been at least three or four feet in height; there were no curtains at the window, but there were fat planked wooden shutters thrown back on either side of it, and it seemed to function as an impromptu door out to the wide front porch.

Varied and intriguing works of art filled all four walls. Both sideboards were covered with a gamut of pottery and sculpture. Despite the strong smells of pancakes, ground coffee, smoky bacon, and freshly sliced oranges just feet away, the entire room had a sort of under-taste of oil paints and wet clay. And on top of it all was a layer of warm morning sounds: a clock ticking languidly against the wall, forks clicking against plates, slow conversation and occasional laughter that was still husky from sleep, the soft padding of bare feet and dog tails thumping on tiled floors.

Wade was trying to take it all in, impression after impression, but Kit had already preceded him into the kitchen beyond, and he felt compelled to follow, so he pushed through to the next room.

The moment Wade stepped through the door into Roddy's kitchen, he felt as if he had come home – not as if he had returned home, but as if he had found the one he had been seeking. There was a sense of peace, a sense of belonging, that he had not felt in a very long time, that he was not sure he had ever felt. He somehow sensed everything about the place, everything about Roddy. It was as if he had been drifting through all of his travels and experiences and living day to day, until he had come to this place and this time. Kit introduced them, but Wade was quite sure that he already knew Roddy like an old soul, a great friend from somewhere before childhood, one to whom he was connected by the universe since before either of them were born. He wasn't sure that he believed in such things; and he feared that perhaps it was just the effect of being in Taos – the energy, the enigma, that was Taos – built, they said, over the earth's invisible "ley lines," which accounted for its influence and pull on some people, especially the natives, those who had a deep and long respect for the earth and could feel its urging, its compelling call. And so it was with great gratitude and reassurance that Wade would learn as time progressed that these feelings in him did not dissipate in the least, but would, in fact, grow stronger, surer.

As she worked around the kitchen, the gold in Roddy's light brown hair kept shifting places like the sun under a summer tree. And she kept having to push it out of her eyes, which were nearly the same brown, ringed with nearly the same gold. She wore her rather significant intelligence quietly, non-threateningly, but it was easily brought out when needed for argument or banter. Raised by a teacher mother and a father in the Secret Service, she had opinions on vast amounts of subjects. She dressed only in natural fabrics, thought underwear was unnatural, wore flowers tucked into her hair or button holes until they wilted and fell apart. She gave feelings to inanimate objects and had favorites. Her elbows and chin and hair usually wore the colors of her current work in progress, and she cooked amazing meals from nearly nothing – primarily by intuition and taste. She was kind beyond reason, loyal without question, thoughtful before speaking, generous and wise to her friends, and unwilling to tolerate any kind of racism or exclusion or inequality or stupidity in people or practices. She expressed herself in her painting, mostly. And in her politics. And in who she chose to love. Both Kit and Wade watched her move and listened to her laugh and both were deeply, madly, grateful for her.

  Just then, two of the other guests, accompanied by the three oversized house dogs, entered the kitchen to fill their plates and they were all introduced to the newcomers. They politely said hello, and with equal politeness tried to ignore the over-ripe smell and look of the new arrivals. The one exception to this show of civility was New-Dog-Lois.

  New-Dog-Lois was the newest addition to the dog contingency of the household (and would be so identified forever after). She had, therefore, never met Kit on his earlier visits, and she was completely smitten with him. She refused to stop sniffing greedily at both men, but it was Kit to whom she repeatedly returned, sighing softly, drooling down his leg. Kit was happy to be in the company of dogs again, and so he petted and rubbed New-Dog-Lois with enthusiasm, scratching her ears and under her chin with a practiced touch, until she finally slid to the floor in what appeared to be a dead faint.

"Is she okay?" Kit asked.

"Oh, yes," Roddy assured him. "She just really likes you. She has no self-control, no self-respect. No class." New-Dog-Lois groaned softly.

Stepping carefully over the prone dog, Roddy finished refilling the large serving platers on her kitchen table and explained, "We're eating late today because it's Sunday. I try to make a sort of brunch on Sundays. So it worked out well for your arrival."

It was tradition for the guests (residents and meal-only patrons alike) to help themselves in the mornings – coming into the kitchen as they arrived, picking up plates and forks, knives and napkins, filling their cups with hot steaming coffee or tea, and then taking their food into the dining room or out onto the front porch. But before they left the kitchen, or as they returned their plates to the sink and resumed their work in their small corner studios and outdoor easels and pottery kilns, they would drop what money they could into a glass jar placed discreetly on the end of one of the kitchen countertops. Those who had nothing to give were never turned away. It was understood that everyone paid what and when they could. It was a system that worked well in this community of generosity and equality.

"The morning meal is a rather casual affair here," Roddy said as she encouraged Kit and Wade to second and third helpings. "We do a bit more of a together thing for supper. You're on your own for lunches."

The men had remained standing, leaning against the kitchen counters while they ate, with New-Dog-Lois seated firmly on Kit's left foot. But Roddy suggested they all go out to the back porch steps – into the fresh air – to finish their coffee. And in that brief breath of a movement – stepping through the open arched doorway onto the stone back steps of Roddy's house – Kit lurched off the edge of time; he was back on the wooden stairs behind the old Fort Wayne apartment house, sitting there with Bruno, watching and aching over the tattered wings of a broken butterfly. He threw his head back and looked up to the window above, perhaps to catch a glimpse of a movement, a shadow, a secret, waiting for him, watching him. And it made him dizzy and he wavered on his feet, he dropped his coffee, and he was ashamed. And then, out of that vortex of time, he heard Bruno's voice saying in all its deliberate, accented tones: … *yes, Christopher, you will fly … the holes will fly with you … but you will fly …* And then it became Wade's voice saying with its familiarity and sureness: "Hey, Buddy … you almost went flying … here, sit down … take my coffee."

As Roddy returned to the kitchen to get fresh coffee for them all, Wade looked Kit in the face and said with deep kindness: "You're really tired, Kit … you're just really tired." New-Dog-Lois licked Kit's hand with uncanny empathy.

☾

"You'll be wanting baths," Roddy stated when they had finished their meal, and then added diplomatically, "I wonder if you'd like to use the outside showers ... at least to begin with. They're quite lovely in the mornings. I'll bring you towels. You can leave me your clothes, ... and we'll deal with them later, yes?" She left them little choice, but both men were quite agreeable to it.

The outside showers were very much open air, with simple exposed pipes of separate hot and cold running water mixing together into a blend of sensations as it spilled across their naked bodies; a few short opaque plastic panels surrounded them for a minimum of decency. It was an experience of absolute freedom and sensual revival. Two of the dogs began to splash and dance in the runoff water (channeled into a pool and saved for the plants). New-Dog-Lois, however, just stared lovingly at Kit and then decided to join him in his shower. It took a couple of thorough sudsings, but the fresh mineral-filled well water eventually worked its way through the thick sludge of dirt, sweat, and wear that covered them from head to foot; and it soothed the beaten places the trains had repeatedly thrown them against, and where the hard ground upon which they had slept rubbed them raw. Roddy found them some temporary clothing, loaned from other guests or things that had been left behind – "house clothes" she called them. They sort of fit and were clean and soft and felt like heaven itself.

While the men showered and toweled down and dressed, Roddy kept up a constant barrage of questions for them – how and where and what next sort of things. And she laughed with them, and was quiet with them. And then, noting their utter exhaustion, she took them to spare rooms at the back of the second floor of the main house, her house. Wade slept for more than twelve hours and woke to the middle of the night, anxious to reassure himself that he was still there; he tossed a bit and then went down to the porch to watch the sun come up and to watch for Roddy to come back into the kitchen. Kit slept for closer to twenty hours and dreamed dreams and saw visions and awoke far after sunrise. New-Dog-Lois never left his side.

☽

Climbing slowly out of bed and over a collapsed dog, Kit went to the open window. He could hear voices, quite sure they were Roddy and Wade. Roddy was taking some clothes down from a long laundry line, Wade helping and hindering her. Kit called a greeting down to them, and they both looked up with wide smiles.

"She boiled our clothes," Wade called up. "Actually boiled them. With lye soap and a wooden butter churn spoon."

"I couldn't think of anything else to do with them," Roddy responded with good humor.

"She was afraid to burn them – releasing all those toxins into this beautiful, clear desert air," Wade continued. "And she refused to put them into the trash."

"We have strict codes about waste and recycling here … I feared for the environment," Roddy responded. "I thought about burying them … but we have coyotes, and I was afraid they or the dogs might dig them up again … and I knew nothing would ever grow over that spot."

"So, in the end," Wade concluded, "she took them to the back of her property, put them in a large pot over an open fire, and just boiled the crap out of them."

"Literally … the crap," Roddy agreed.

"You're a brave woman," Kit called down as New-Dog-Lois joined him in the widow opening. "A brave and wise and good woman. How can we repay you?"

"Oh, you will."

"By the way, I called Zanna," Roddy continued to tell Kit. "Told her you're here and safe. But I also told her I think you should – and will – stay here for another few days or so and rest up. Come on down and get some breakfast."

"But I just ate breakfast," Kit said as an aside to New-Dog-Lois, "… and yet … I am that hungry again."

Days and nights slipped past them, somehow, without effort or explanation. Time had not stopped, but it no longer mattered. In its place was an easy comfortable routine, that felt to Kit like listening to a lover's breathing as she fell asleep against the curve of his back. But the lover was not Suzanna. And so they stayed in Taos yet another night and day and night and day, until they stopped counting them.

Wade completed painting the trim on the main house, although he secretly preferred it as the unfinished portrait it had been. And he began to work on the fencing.

Kit took comfort in the kitchen, cooking, cleaning up, discovering new vegetarian culinary skills; while New-Dog-Lois never wavered in her adoration and insistence on keeping company with him.

Some afternoons, on a borrowed guitar on the back steps of the house, Kit and Wade wrote the songs they had promised they would, and played many they already knew, and rewrote the ones they thought they remembered; and then they performed them for an enthusiastic, growing audience in the evenings on Roddy's front porch. Recognition of Kit Williams was high in this community, and the news of his presence spread quickly.

One day, Wade found a darkroom in town that he could borrow and he developed the most recent photos he had taken – mostly of Kit and Roddy, and the artists and the Pueblo natives and the other locals, and the dogs and cats and burros and additional assorted animals; the majority of the film containing the railroad tramps had already been sent to a friend in Chicago for processing and safekeeping, according to his original plans. Kit and Roddy and all those who viewed this work were greatly taken by Wade's brilliant, yet unheralded talent. When Wade first spread the prints across the dining room table, Kit studied them long and hard and eventually realized that he couldn't find his own face, until Wade pointed it out to him. In it, he saw what Wade saw; and it was just another stranger.

      The autumn Taos nights were cool, with grand skies that had no beginning or ending or measure or equal, presenting a vast saga of stars and moon and unimagined possibilities. Long into these nights, Wade and Roddy would talk and share their stories with each other, with laughter and truth and a sense of meaningfulness. And long into these nights, Kit would run – with his own sense of meaningfulness, his own truth.

Kit began his ritual of night running between Roddy's house and the town plaza. He slipped out silently, leaving New-Dog-Lois to wait up for him, which she was delighted to do. He had decided to run with moccasined feet. And so, night after night, he learned and relearned the feel of the ground beneath him; the roll of each foot, the pressure and balance, the give and resistance. Then he recalled the memory of rhythm – his legs and arms and breathing in sync with time and space. Then he no longer needed to remember it, or to even think about it, he just felt it. And he began going out into the desert. Every night, farther and farther. He skimmed the scrub and darted through the trees as if he had grown up with them, or grown out of them. He felt the moon as it followed him, showing him his way. He raced against the "mountains of blood" themselves, and they seemed to wait for him. He saw the rabbits dance at his coming, the mice hold fast, the owls pay him tribute with their turning heads and mirror-backed eyes, silencing their hunting cries until he had passed. And his legs were no longer muscle and bone and skin, they were simply sound as they stroked the ground – thud-skiff, thud-skiff, thud-skiff, thud-skiff – like a heart beating, his heart, speaking to the earth. And the earth urged him on as if he were running home again. And he could see the old apartment house up ahead – shadowed, defined only by the moon. He could see his mother's light from her window and he was running toward it. But it shifted and smudged and went dim, as the moon's face was suddenly blinded behind the hands of a cloud, and it was not the old house, it was the ancient pueblo dwellings north of the town. The Taos pueblo community, compelling and mysterious.

Kit's stride slowed as he approached it. The moon had returned and in its light the main pueblo dwelling was all edges and angles, given shape and dimension only by its own shadows. And he saw for the first time how much a part of the land it was – not so much rising up from it as it was resting against its lap, leaning into its breast. He counted five distinct stories at its highest point. And each level seemed to spread and sigh as it came closer to the very earth from which it was made.

All around its perimeter there stood jagged roughwood drying racks, built for the hunts – for curing meat and hanging skins, now empty, with only a few occasional thin strands of pale wool floating out from their arms like memories being forgotten. And there was the sound of the river living nearby – rushing in spring thaws, slowing in summer droughts, now resting yet restless within its autumn bed.

He saw how grand and yet homely the pueblo was, constantly touched and worn by life for longer than a millennium, protecting its people, giving birth and heritage to them, grieving their deaths, one generation after another after another. And he could feel its great age emanating from it; he could understand its ancient traditions – why it still refused the use of electricity and running water; he could hear the whispers of its ancient secrets. And at its back, he believed in the talisman of Taos Mountain as it rose up, protective, watchful, guarding.

And so he stood very still in the quiet and watched the old pueblo as it moved and shifted and breathed with the night. And then he sat down, and he breathed in a faint scent of woodsmoke and sage on the night air; and he laid down, spreading himself flat against the ground, beneath the cover of stars, and he waited for something, without knowing what.

What came to him were dreams. Dreams that crept in with silent footfalls. Dreams that were more like visions intertwined with memories and things yet to be. Dreams that were completely experiential, involving all his senses. He heard the cry of wolves and the gruff moan of the bear, the splashing of waters, the voices of women singing in the backs of their throats. He felt the cross poles of pueblo ladders beneath his feet and within his hands as he climbed up and over the walls of an adobe dwelling that had no windows and no doors along any of its walls. He smelled burning grasses and roasting food. And at the apex of the dreams there was a young native boy who called Kit "Running Fox," and then laughed and hid himself in the shadows and then ran away. The boy was perhaps nine or ten years of age, with beautifully browned skin, untamed black hair, and a familiarity about him that Kit was unable to recall. His clothing was torn and dirty, as though he'd been lying in dirt and weeds for a long time, and he was too thin, too desperate, somehow. But his eyes were clear and clever and full of humor; and Kit wanted to tell him to be careful and be safe, but he was no longer in sight. Also within the center of the dreams was a very old woman who seemed as aged as the pueblo itself. She was dressed in all-white regalia, including the blanket that lay across her right shoulder and breast and tucked through her belt and swung down to touch the thick animal-hide leggings that covered her lower legs. Her hair was perfectly white as well, and as ethereal as the moon, still thick as a young girl's, braided and smooth, like strings of fat pearls falling down her back. She was small and straight and graceful. Her face was deeply tanned with sun, deeply etched with time. Her eyes were black, shining, polished onyx, yet soft and terribly wise; eyes that saw everything and understood more. She had taken Kit's hand, as if to lead him someplace, and he noticed the feel of her hand in his: tiny-boned yet strong; and he could see her pulse, beating purple in the thinness between her thumb and forefinger. She told him her name was Aponi. And she sat down beside him, and she listened to his spirit, and she told him sacred stories.

      But just as she was finishing one story that seemed to be of great importance and meaning to him, her voice began breaking apart and fading away, sliding into pink light, and he could no longer understand her words. He was trying to make his way closer to her, and his eyes were blinded by the light, and he shut them tightly, and then opened them to the dawn sun stretching awake across the mountains.

      He could hear the early stirrings of morning life coming from the pueblo, inside it, around it; dogs greeting the day, sheep bawling to be fed, hushed human voices using words he couldn't discern. He rose from the ground, chilled and stiff, and he looked all around where he stood for the young laughing boy who had hidden from him and the old woman in white who was telling him the story he needed still to hear; he even began walking toward the pueblo buildings to try to seek them out. But he knew he wouldn't find them. And suddenly he felt ashamed and confused and like an intruder in a sacred space. And so he turned away. He started walking, then running, tracing his own footprints back to Roddy's. The sun was racing at his heels, trying to catch him, trying to pass him by.

"There you are," Roddy greeted Kit as he came into the kitchen through the back porch door." She was just starting breakfast. "Grab a bowl … start scrambling," she said with a smile, handing him a wire basket full of fresh eggs. Her eyes were carefully taking him in. "It's nice to have some quiet one-to-one time with you."

Kit had still not answered her, although he had washed his hands and was whisking eggs, shaking in salt and pepper and a bit of rosemary and other seasonings, freshly cut or dried and hanging overhead. His mind was still a mile out into the desert.

Roddy remained quiet, giving him the space to fill for himself, if he chose.

And then he began: "I've been running again. At night. Into the desert. But I suppose you know that," he looked over at her. Of course Roddy knew, and she nodded at him.

"I ran to the old Taos Pueblo last night."

Roddy remained silent but obviously attentive.

"Wow - hard to put this into words," Kit tried again. "I wasn't smoking anything …"

At this, Roddy laughed out loud. "And yet, you had an experience," she finally helped him along.

"And yet, I did."

"Good … bad … ?"

"I don't know, exactly," Kit replied truthfully and with slight humor. "But I was hoping I could talk to you about it. Hoping you might be able to help me make sense of it."

"Of course, Sweetie. Let's get everybody fed, and then take a long walk together. Try to keep remembering all the details. And watch your eggs ... they're going a bit brownish ..."

As soon as breakfast was consumed and cleared and Wade was left with the washing up, Kit and Roddy gathered all the dogs and started walking toward the old Taos Plaza. Kit replayed the entire night for Roddy, beginning with his run in the desert all the way to the pueblo, and how he had felt the pull and influence of the singular desert night, its almost shamanistic, spiritual, effects. He told her how he had rested and waited and then began to see and hear and smell the night, the fragrance of smudging pots, the rushing of the river, the heartbeat of the earth itself. And he told her about the child – the boy – in as much detail as he could hold on to about his look and actions, the sound of his laughter, how he had called Kit "Running Fox," but then had run away from him and hidden in the shadows. And he told her of the old woman, wise and beautiful and intriguing, dressed all in white, and about her eyes, and about her words and her stories, and how she had said her name was Aponi. He remembered telling the woman things about himself, but he wasn't sure what they were. And he tried to repeat her exact telling of her stories and how she talked to him of the animals and the rocks, the clouds and the collective memory of her people. But by then he realized it was starting to be available to him only in scraps and bits, flashes and torn images. And he knew he was forgetting too much of it, aware that it was slipping away from him, like dreams in the early morning or reflections in the background of mirrors and empty store windows. He kept grasping at it all, trying to make it into memory and experience and not so dream-like. But it was becoming too fragile, too elusive, like the mere suggestive sound of a single bar of music, or the vague memory of a favorite book read long ago, the aftertaste of a last kiss. The feelings from it all were easily recalled, but not the actual experience. And he shared his fear and frustration of forgetting with Roddy.

"But now that you've told it to me, we can both keep it safe," she reassured him. "And I have a suggestion that might help. You've heard the talk about the San Geronimo Feast Day that starts tomorrow; there will be a great deal of activity taking place out at the old Taos Pueblo all day – ceremonies and dancing and foot races and storytelling, that sort of thing. There may be something that will connect with you out there – perhaps even some of the native Indians will be willing to talk to you about it. Lots of our artists will be showing their work there. In fact, I have a good friend who's a potter – and a meal patron of mine – who was born in the old pueblo. We can talk to her tonight after dinner, if you'd like. I can ask her."

The evening meal was done and cleared. The sky was very high with late light and first stars, swept clear by the clouds that leaned, brush-edged, against the west. Roddy shepherded Kit and Wade and her friend Anita out to the back steps of the house, along with a large pitcher of Sangria, which had been prepared for the next day's Festival, but brought out early just for them.

The pitcher was gracefully and rather sensuously shaped pottery, heavy and plump, deep red, unglazed and beautifully decorated. "That's one of mine, isn't it?" Anita remarked.

"Of course," Roddy said. "One of the best things about being surrounded by my talented artisans is the beauty they leave in their wake."

Kit had brought out his good cigars for the occasion, too, and all four of them filled the air with their aromatic smoke and silence.

Crickets and coyotes started to speak to the night first. And then, in rushes of memory, interrupted with moments of silence, Kit related his experience in the desert the night before to Anita and Wade.

When he seemed to be finished, Anita broke the final silence by saying: "Well, let me begin by saying that you were in sacred space that near the pueblo, and last night our men were in the Kiva with their prayers – that's a ceremonial place of importance to the village – so I would counsel you to believe in the visions, in the experience. I don't think it was simply a dream. And, anyway, I'm not an interpreter of dreams. But I can tell you of the symbolism, according to my people, perhaps give you a place where you can build your own insight and understanding of what you experienced. Is that good?"

Kit nodded, so Anita continued: "First, the woman's name, Aponi, means butterfly, if that has any significance to you." Kit's heart thudded heavily at the word butterfly and pieces of thoughts broke into him:

> Bruno and the butterfly ... the old house steps ... the pieces torn away ... but still she flew ... still she flew ... the Mexican butterflies ... the windshield, broken and smashed ... a gunshot ... I will fly ...

And he heard Anita's voice: "... but the name Aponi is Blackfoot, not Tanoan – not from the Taos pueblo people. In fact, our language is never shared outside the community. A few of our members still speak it, and it's being taught again – but only in the tradition of strict secrecy and sacredness. In fact, the whole idea of identity is kept very discreetly in our culture – only to oneself ... "

> Don't tell, don't ... never talk about it ... never talk about your mother, your father, your family ... our secrets ... keep it to ourselves ... punishment if you tell ... can't be loved if you tell ...

And it was Roddy's voice saying: "... I would guess that the young boy probably called Kit 'Running Fox' just as a double meaning for 'kit' – meaning a young fox – and the fact that Kit had just been actually running. So maybe that part's not too hard to interpret – yes?"

Anita agreed. "But there is a breed of foxes in this area called 'Kit Foxes.' They are excellent runners, all foxes are, often tirelessly. But more than that, the fox holds deeper meaning and significance to the Indians. For instance, it's usually a sign of living by means of cleverness and cunning, learning to make one's way around difficulties or obstacles in life, rather than addressing them head on ..."

> Syphon gas, don't buy it ... always please your mother, your teachers, the priest ... do what you're told ... come out of the water ... drugs are easier, easier ... stay back stage, stay back ... take the tires, take the lead, take the gig, take the weed ... run, run faster...

" ... which is not a bad life skill to have, I think. And the fox is considered to be strong in feminine magic and shapeshifting or invisibility – which is really just a form of camouflage, fitting in with your surroundings or being unseen when you want. Foxes are really great at that ..."

> Behind the refrigerator ... out of sight ... I have a good friend who lives under the stairs ... hide, hide so no one can find you ... change your skin color ... shapeshift, color shift ... be the other boy ... be the best boy, sing the solo, hide in plain sight ...

"... and foxes are very liminal, too – especially Kit Foxes. They live almost entirely in that time between night and day, between the realms of reality ..."

>Two boys ... one skin ... one good boy ... the splinters are getting sharp ... there is no reflection, no photograph ... good boy, bad boy, day boy, night boy ...

" ... so it's all very spiritual." Anita stopped for a moment and consulted her memory for more. "Foxes are great swimmers, too, although they hate the water – and that's interpreted to mean that they don't want to return to the feminine waters of life they came from ..."

>Rio Grande ... Rio Bravo ... bravo, bravo ... encore, one more, one more ... swim for it ... run for it ... sing for it ... FBI Flores ... pink shoes ... get out of the water ... stop swimming ... just stop ...

" ... but they will swim if they have to, if they have to save themselves. Oh – and I love this bit – they have a trait, a way of acting, that's actually called 'charming' – used like a verb. It's like a dance they do, they act playful and lighthearted, and it allows them to attract – or 'charm' – the things they want without showing their true desires or intention – their true 'need,' I guess you could call it."

> Sorry ... I'm sorry ... Suzanna's
> leaving ... before I loved her,
> it was easy ... but she's too close now
> ... too close, too loved, too connected
> ... I love her too much ... it's just
> too much ... I'm sorry ...
> just don't leave ...

Kit suddenly became aware that Anita had stopped talking and they were all looking at him. But he couldn't yet speak. And then Anita took pity on him and she added: "The fact that the old woman disappeared into the sunrise – into the East – is indicative of new beginnings, healing, creativity, learning, that kind of thing; and the white of her attire and hair and all is generally pretty much what you'd think – purity, truth – but it can also indicate a scattering or splintering of something ... or of someone." And then she slapped her knees with both hands and said: "So, there you go, that's about all I can tell you. Does any of that help?"

Kit nodded silently, thoughtfully, and he thanked her for sharing her culture and insight. And he excused himself without looking at any of them and he went upstairs to his bedroom and he closed his door in the dark. He did not want the light. He lay on the bed with New-Dog-Lois at his side, her head heavy across his chest, sharing his heartbeats, and he did not sleep for a long time. He felt he had been found out, somehow, exposed. And he felt relieved.

☾

"**Get up.** We need to be leaving now if we're going to watch the foot races at the pueblo." Kit was in Wade's room, turning on lights and directing New-Dog-Lois to get on the other man's bed and sit on him. It was less than a hour before sunrise.

"Was that me who said I was going to go with you? I could swear it was Roddy," Wade mumbled.

"I've made coffee. You can pick it up as you go through the kitchen. I'll meet you down there – and I'll be leaving in about twenty minutes."

"Take the dog … please … take the dog … I'll be down in a minute."

Wade was true to his word and they headed off into the dark, headed the way Kit was used to running. Kit had to remind himself to quiet his heart, slow his body, to walk a normal pace with his two friends beside him – Wade on one side, New-Dog-Lois on the other. The dog was alert to every sound and shape and scent around them, and she moved with the attitude of being one of the chosen.

Wade, too, breathed in the predawn freshness and watched the shadows form and fade as they made their way north. "This feels familiar … walking in the early-morning next to you … out in the middle of nowhere … just without the backpacks and bedrolls," he observed. The air almost had a taste to it, succulent, new, just released from the plants and earth around them. A coolness was blowing out of the south.

"Thanks for coming with me," Kit said. "I haven't watched a foot race in a long time. I think the last time was the final race where I watched my friend Jacob win … the last one he ran …" And they fell silent for awhile.

The ceremonial races ahead of them were to begin at dawn and all the participants were men and all wore only breechclouts – material made of tanned deerskins or woven cloth and folded with tradition under and around their loins, just like all the generations before them. It would be the inaugural event of the day; a day that would be lived with ceremony and history, heritage and spirituality.

Wade had been sorry to learn that no cameras were allowed at the pueblo for any part of the day. No visual recordings, no voice recordings. Visitors and participants would capture the experience in their hearts and minds alone, and they would remember it all, the smells and sights, the people, the conversations, the stories, the sense of place and being, all the meaning and energy of it, as it was meant to be known and remembered and understood, from an individual perspective, a personal interpretation, of a community shared.

The closer they got to the pueblo, the more people were joining them, all hushed with respect and anticipation. It was that liminal time of deep blue when Kit felt most at home and to which he seemed most connected. The sun was beginning to join them as well, creeping up the mountains on the backs of shadows.

The races were primitive and thrilling. Kit's legs and heart and breath remembered it all. And he watched the surrounding crowds for the faces of mothers, and he tried to pick them out, one from the next. He looked for Jacob's mother among them.

The sun was gaining height as Roddy came and found them. Anita was there, and many of the other artists Kit and Wade knew from Roddy's compound. They all wandered the art displays and the tables of traditional handcrafts and shared the food that the people had prepared. And Kit began to separate himself from the others, keeping only the dog at his side. He searched for the young boy and the woman in white; but their images had faded into mere sketches in his mind until he doubted if he would recognize them. But still he searched.

He watched the ceremonial dances and let the music carry him up the mountains and into the caves and the drums haunted his heart and the men's voices sang to a terrible emptiness in him – a truth he didn't want to hear.

In the late afternoon, Kit was caught up by Anita and she led him to a table of beautiful turquoise jewelry that her husband had made. But just at that moment, the air was cracked and seared with a mad howling, unearthly baying, coming from above them, coming from all around them. Everything stopped, everything held its breath, everything held its words and music and bartering and laughing and eating and telling each other things. The children were the first to move and ran shrieking to their mothers' skirts. Kit looked to Anita's face and found she showed surprise, but was smiling as well. She pointed to the roofs of the pueblo buildings behind them just as ten men all leapt to the ground, shouting and stunning in their appearance and action. They wore thick stripes of black and white paint from their feet up to their hair, which was parted in the middle, done up in bunches at either side of their heads and wrapped tightly with cornhusks. Black paint encircled their eyes and mouths, making their tongues appear overly red and wet and laughing.

"It's the Koshares, the Kossas some call them, the sacred clowns," she spoke near Kit's ear to be heard over the shouts and loud prattle of the men. "They're like the medieval European court jesters who make social commentary and ease tensions in the community with humor. Some call them 'Delight Makers' – but they're very much tricksters – so watch out. See how the merchants have covered over their wares? These guys will walk by and swipe things that catch their eye – so they're offered other things for free, like candy and cigarettes and beads."

As Anita gestured to the clowns making their way through the festival, Kit saw them prance and stomp and taunt individuals in the crowd – mostly children – but very intimidating to even the most experienced elders.

Kit felt unaccountably drawn to them, familiar with them. And his mind slid back to a jail cell in Texas and he said under his breath: *Santiago ... Marco.*

"It's important for these men to lose their own identities behind the identity of the Koshares, so that they are able to tell the truth of things that may not be pleasant for the hearer to receive," Anita continued to explain. "But you are just as likely to get dunked in the river by one of them, or made to race with them or watch them dance."

Oh yes ... Kit knew them, and he laughed.

"But the best part is that at some point this afternoon, they'll have a greased-pole-climbing contest." Anita pointed to a tall pole erected in the center of the dance plaza for the day. At the very top was fasten the hide of an animal – a sheepskin it looked like to Kit. And it was hanging upside down. And next to it were slung several other bundles. Anita said these contained baked treats and other kinds of food, which would be brought down by the winner at the end of the pole-climbing ceremony, and distributed only among themselves. "The maddening thing is that only the men – the clowns themselves – know when this will happen – it's extremely fun to watch, but it could be hours from now."

Kit watched the clowns and their pretenses, the seriousness of it, the idiocy of it, the need of it, and he watched the flashbacks of Marco and the Mexican backroads and so many other times in his life. And then he grew weary from it, and he took his leave from Anita, and he went looking for the storytellers, with the dog close at his heels.

When he had found the storytelling, he sat on the ground among the listeners, became one of them, unseen, invisible, shapeshifting into the place and its people, and he listened.

The stories enthralled him, enchanted him. These were stories told to the grandmothers and grandfathers, painted on the walls of caves and traced with the movement of the stars, stories etched into the faces of the mountains and held in the hearts of stones, stories written in every curve of the pueblo dwellings, stories remembered by this place, to be recited by its people.

Some of the storytellers talked about the holiness of the ground and its waters and its animals – the silent language of horses, the slyness of coyotes, the music of wolves, the sacredness of eagles, the legends of opossums and snakes and spider webs.

And Kit was reminded of the scantiness of his own life stories. He remembered vaguely about Rene and his French grandparents. He remembered Bruno and the animals. But they were now just slight childhood recollections and a few faded photographs hidden away in the backs of books on his mother's shelves. But they were his and all he had, however woefully unlike these spoken histories of native legacy and wisdom. And so he tried to lean into the pueblo stories hard and take them into himself as his own.

As the day began to fade, a new storyteller took her place among them. She was dressed all in white, but did not look familiar to Kit. And yet, her eyes sought and found him, looked directly at him, and then she shifted her gaze to the sky. The moon was rising and she pointed to it on the horizon. It was a waxing gibbous moon, growing yet not quite full with one side still held back in the dark, a moon that portends change and loss and uncertainty. And it was soft edged and tentative against the still light sky, as if it were made with milk paint. But the woman held it firm in her eyes and began her story with the same question that had been asked of her long, long ago:

> "And do you know why it is that the Moon has but one eye?"
>
> "In the time before time, The Trues, who are the unseen spirits that are above all, made T'hoor-íd-deh, the Sun, to be father of all things, and they made P'áh-hlee-oh, the Moon-Maiden to be the mother of all things; and from them, began all the world and all that is in it; and all their children were strong and good and they were very happy. Sun-Father guarded them by day and the Moon-Mother by night – except there was no night; for at that time the Moon had two eyes, and saw as clearly as the Sun, and with a glance as bright, so all was as one long day of golden light. The birds flew always, the flowers never shut, the young people danced and sang, and none knew how to rest. But at last the Trues realized that the endless light grew heavy to the world's young eyes that knew no tender lids of night. And they said: 'It is not well, for there is no sleep, and the world is very tired. We must not keep the Sun and Moon seeing alike. Let us put out one

of the eyes of the Sun-Father, so that there may be darkness for half the time, and then his children can rest.' But when the Moon-Mother heard it, she cried: 'No! Take my eyes for my children; do not blind the Sun – blind me instead.' And so the Trues agreed and took away one of her eyes, so that she could never see half so well again. And so the night came upon the tired earth, and the flowers and birds and people slept their first sleep, and it was very good. But she who had such love for her children – and paid for them with such pain as mothers pay – she did not grow ugly and unloved by her sacrifice; she became lovelier and more loved, even today; for in place of the bloom of girlhood, the Trues gave her the beauty that is only found in the faces of mothers."

When the woman in white had finished, she looked again at Kit's face. He could somehow feel her hands against his cheeks, cradling him with great tenderness. The sense of her touch was so strong that Kit stood up, nearly falling back, his legs stiff from time sitting, his heart pounding. And then the coolness of an early evening breeze brushed away the warmth of her hands. And he realized she was yards away from him, could not possibly have touched him. And he called to the dog, and he turned and walked away, growing steadier, faster, back toward town, back to Roddy's and a firmer, more familiar reality. But the story told by the woman echoed after him and pursued him. Her words pulled at him, gripping at his shirt, his feet, his ears, his heart.

The moon is the mother.
The mother-moon. Is she my mother?
The moon mother sacrificed for her children, my mother sacrificed for her only child. Were her sacrifices too great? Too much? Too much for her, too much in her own eyes, too much in her own mind, too much in her own life? And the moon became half blind ... half blind ... half blind moon ... half blind mother. She could not see, she would not see, she could not see the pain, she would not see the brokenness ... and the darkness ... she did not see her darkness became her son's darkness. Her darkness, my darkness, shared darkness. It was so dark behind the refrigerator. The mother allowed the son to walk into that darkness with her. Did I walk into that darkness on my own? Why? Why could I never tell the secrets? Forgive the father ... forgive the mother ... forgive the only son.

And so the woman's story trailed behind him, refusing to be unheard or forgotten.

🌙

Kit could see the lights shining out from the back of Roddy's house from quite a distance in the dark, winking, beckoning, into the night. Wade had hung small strings of them across the back porch, its steps and railings, similar to the ones already in place in the front, and it looked like a reflection of the night sky itself, with stars scattered to the ground. But Kit held the moon within himself as he stopped to get his breath before entering their space. He could hear the mix of voices, laughing, the clink of the Sangria pitcher as it was passed.

New-Dog-Lois circled Kit's legs, questioning, urging him, herding him on toward the others. And so he acquiesced, folding the day away, tucking it into his mind and heart for a time when he would spread it out and examine it, later, alone.

"Hey! There you are!" The familiar voices called out to him with great feeling and the warmth of the wine, and they waved him forward. "We looked for you as we left. Couldn't find you."

"I was at the storytelling."

"I said that – didn't I say that?" Wade was confident and feeling the drink.

"Here's a glass for you … the Sangria is cold and lovely," Roddy said as she came out of the back door, lifting a pottery cup high over her head in a salute to him. "But first … the phone just rang, did you hear it ring? It's Zanna. She said to come get you, she's waiting, on the phone. Go talk to Zanna. I will hold your wine for you."

Kit ran up the steps two at a time and into the kitchen – to the nearest phone extension in the house. "Suzanna? Hi. Yeah – just walked in from the Festival out at the old pueblo. You should have been there. I've got so much to tell you. I've got so much …"

"Wait, Kit … I'm in New York. I just got in myself from the airport, I flew back from Aspen tonight. And I got a call, or rather you got a call."

Neither of them interrupted the silence.

"Kit – it's your mom. I'm so sorry. She passed away night-before-last. It was in her sleep … probably a stroke … she wasn't in any pain. But they couldn't reach either of us. They've been trying. But I just got the call … it's the only number they had. I'm so sorry, Kit. I'm so terribly sorry."

And the moon turned over inside him and it fell out of the sky.

☾

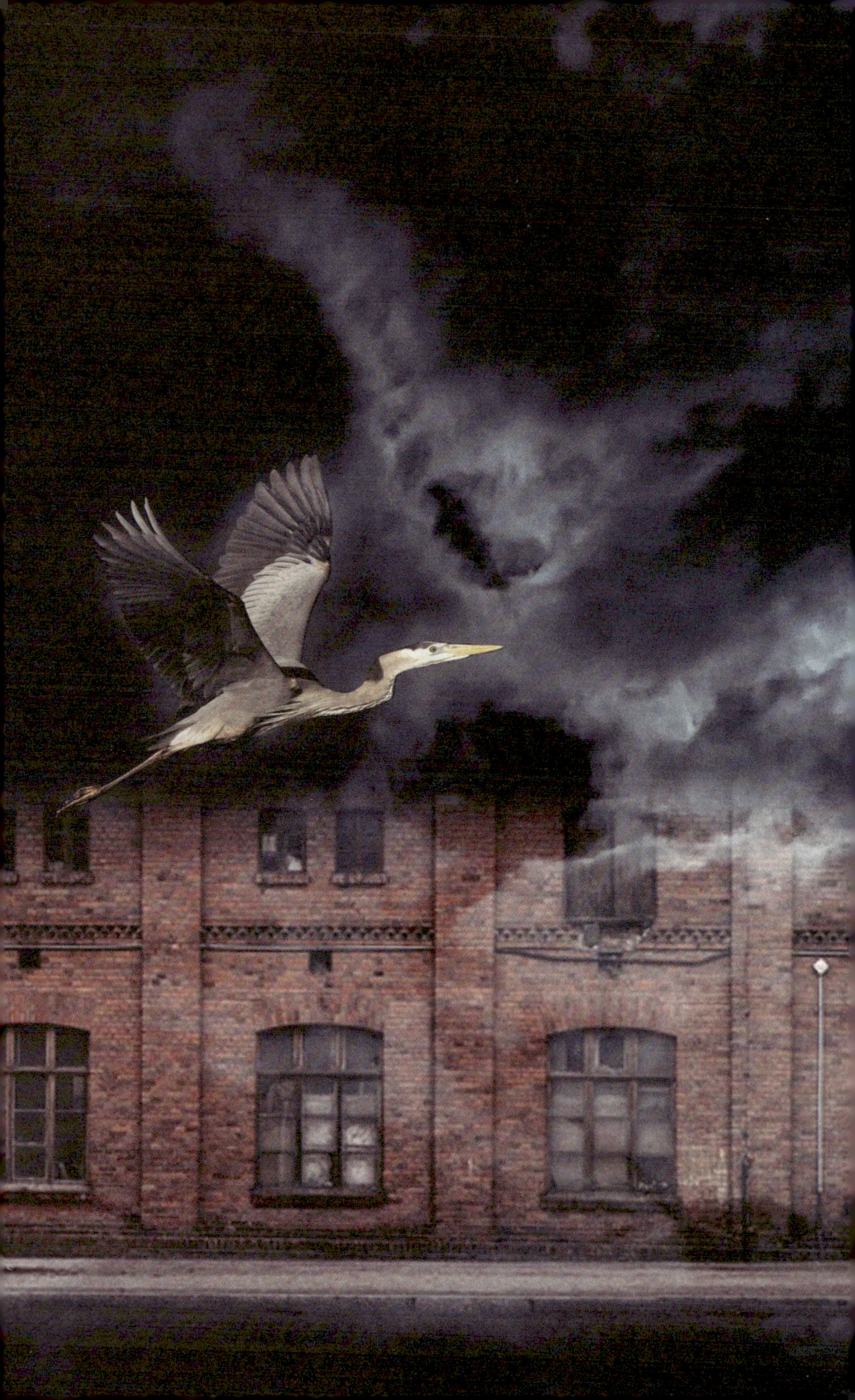

PART FIVE

Going Home.

October 1, 1972 -
September 29, 1978

They said goodbye as if it were for the last time and promised each other that it wouldn't be. But the bus was waiting for him. And Fort Wayne was waiting for him. And his mother was waiting for him.

    The cold air that morning after the Festival came out of the north and west with a sort of arrogance, as it shoved and jostled the early October warmth out of its way, spreading and settling itself across the old bare feet of the mountains. Kit shivered slightly and pulled his least favorite sweater up higher across the back of his neck. He watched the bus as it began to creak against the weight of strangers and their suitcases, some with bundles tied in thin ropes and rough knots, along with their private sadness and anticipation and indifference. He handed his own baggage to the driver to load in along with everyone else's.

    Roddy and Wade and New-Dog-Lois had walked with him to the Plaza bus stop, and Anita was rushing up to them just then, too, breathless, her shoulders hidden beneath her blanket. They all stood without words for a few minutes. Kit crouched and rubbed his face against New-Dog-Lois's neck one last time. They had spent enough time together for the animal to read him and to know. Instinctively, the dog went and sat behind Roddy's legs, looking away from Kit with intentionality.

    Roddy was handing Kit a weighty, bulging brown paper grocery sack, its top rolled down tightly, and she was explaining the food inside, because she knew he had spent close to his last forty dollars for the bus ticket back to Indiana. She said there were sandwiches and oranges and other things that should hold him for the entire twenty-hour, thousand-mile trip without spoiling; a thermos of hot coffee she thought would get him as far as Kansas City; some of her homemade "Hojarascas," the Mexican shortbread cookies for which Kit had acquired a serious affection, that he could never make quite the same way she did. "And I've rather forgotten what else," she tried to laugh.

"And there's one more thing inside," she said as she touched the sides of the sack gently with both hands. "You can open it on the road. Or wait until you get home. I've written you a note about it."

"Here's something from me, too," Anita handed him a small package, carefully wrapped in burlap and tied with cornhusks. "It's for your mother – in remembrance of her, in honor of her," she said looking Kit in his eyes as deeply as he would let her. "It's called Mah-pah-róo, and it is the most sacred charm of my people – the most beautiful. It represents the Moon Mother – the most beautiful of all women – who gave up her sight for her children. It was probably one of the stories you heard at the Festival. Anyway, it's made using a single flawless ear of pure white corn, which represents fertility and motherhood, and it's decorated all over with snow-white feathers and with bits of silver and coral and precious turquoise." She motioned to the package with her long brown fingers as she talked. "You may have seen some representations of her during some of the dances yesterday, too. But this one was made just for you, just for you and your mother. Jacob and I made it for you last night." Kit's head snapped up at the mention of "Jacob," and then he remembered that it was Anita's husband's name. She laid the gift in his open hand, and closed his fingers around it, cupping her own hands around his warmly. And then she smiled and stepped back from him, and he tucked the gift into his pocket closest to his heart.

    Kit found just enough of his voice to thank both the women for all they had given him – not just then, and not just for the food and the wrapped mementos. He needed them to understand how much meaning their lives held for him. Their love and tenderness when he needed it. Their insightfulness. Their grace. To Anita he said that he would never forget her or her people and her culture and hospitality, and he held her against his chest. And to Roddy he said: "I will always be indebted to Suzanna for bringing you into my life – you know that. If for no other thing – and there are literally thousands of things – for that one above all else I will never be able to thank her enough. You are the wisest and kindest …" and he reached for her, but Roddy simply laid her fingers against her lips, letting her tears fall between them. And then she turned away from him, and New-Dog-Lois followed her.

    Wade remained. And he stayed with Kit until he was on the bus. He reached up and tapped on the window glass beside Kit's face.

    Kit waited until he was more than an hour into the trip before he finally opened his curled fist and looked at the gift Wade had pressed into it when he had clasped his hand in a final parting, as they had hugged and clapped each other's shoulders without words.

The bus had stopped twice for fuel and for the driver to take a break, as well as for them all to stretch their legs and use the local bathrooms. Once had been in Colorado and the second in Kansas, both in towns so small and so isolated that there was no chance of any of the passengers making a run for it, Kit kept thinking. And he remembered the times he and Wade had used such places in desperation for bits of dirty soap and lukewarm water. It was less than a month ago and it was a lifetime ago. And sometimes he dozed and awoke with a start as the bus rattled in a particular way – and he pulled at the chains on his wrists and was surprised when they jerked freely. It was less than three months ago and it was a lifetime ago.

When they reached Kansas City, it was after sunset but still early. He had eaten most of the food and had shared oranges with the woman in the seat next to him. She was young and had a baby boy with her that she nursed discreetly and frequently so that it never cried and mostly slept. Kit remembered sharing oranges with strangers another time in a rail yard – another very long time ago.

They boarded a new driver at that stop. He seemed relaxed but overly cheerful and he introduced himself as Ed and made sure everyone was seated and comfortable and having a good time before he started them off on the last half of the journey.

Within a few hours, they were far from any large cities and it was deeply dark outside the bus windows, probably near midnight, Kit estimated, but he didn't really care. Outside, they were passed by the stream and blur of the head- and taillights of just a few random cars every now and again, while the only lights inside the bus were along the floorboards, at the edges of their scuffed shoes and restless feet, with another half a dozen oval shaped opaque shades that glowed on each side wall every few rows. But even that subdued lighting made it hard to see out of the windows past his own reflection, which looked double edged and ghosted, almost wire-meshed. And the reflections bothered him, irritated him, tried to influence his thoughts and memories.

  And so Kit looked away and pulled from his pocket the small bit of polished amethyst that Wade had given him as they had said goodbye. It was a soft oval shape, dipped in the center in the shape of his thumb. A worry stone. He knew that Wade must have bought it at the San Geronimo Festival. And he knew that of all the stones used for this purpose, crystals were the favored, and amethyst the most prized of all because of its reputed inherent ability to bring peace to the holder regardless of its shape. And then the conversation came back to him; a time when he and Wade were still catching out trains and following the tracks, and they had been searching for a safe jungle late in the day. They had passed a place where there were too many men for Wade's comfort, too rough and foul, overly quiet. Wade's instinct told him this was unsafe and to keep moving. And so they walked on as the sky deepened and it had become a remarkable purple in color. And Wade had told Kit about when he was 13 years old and he had been riding his bike home late one evening when it was just coming onto this time of night, this very color. He was late with his paper route and hurrying home, supposed to be in before dark, but a new customer had been slow paying him and had kept him too long and tried to not pay at all, and so Wade had told him stories and made him laugh until the man reached into his pocket and paid him what he was owed. Wade had jumped back onto his bike and leaned into the last turn onto his street and peddled as hard as he could, hoping he would not be in trouble. The car had come up behind him. There had been no horn, no squeal of tires, no sound at all in his memory. He was thrown into a cracking pain that he thought was going to split him in two. Slowly the feeling of the pavement shuddered under him, and sounds were returning, voices calling to him from a very great distance, and he wanted to just shut his eyes and let go. But then he saw the sky and he was caught up in its deep purple and he was floating on its color and within its space, and he knew if he could just focus on it, he could stay alive and he could keep his mind away from the blackness of the pain, he knew it would keep him from sliding over the edge of consciousness and into that darkness. He just had to hold on to the purple sky. It was his touchstone color he said. His saving color. And now Kit would always carry a part of Wade's life and soul with him in this small stone. He turned the stone over and over in his hand and his mind. And then he put it back into his pocket, afraid he might lose it.

 "That's a beautiful palm stone," the woman in the seat next to him said in a low voice, a middle-of-the-night near whisper, almost conspiratorial sounding. "My grandfather called them 'soothing stones.' Were you given that one by your grandfather?" she asked.

 "No … it was a gift from a very good friend of mine," Kit responded, pulling the stone back out again.

"It is tradition in my family that such stones are handed down one generation to the next – so there is a sort of sacred connectedness in them. You will have to keep that dear to you, and give it to your own son one day," she concluded and pressed her son into her breast with a soothing sensualness.

Kit rubbed his thumb across the stone again and felt it grounding him, comforting him, with its intrinsic energy and meaning.

They came to another rest stop. Kit noted that it was going on 1:00 a.m. and they were in Bloomington, Illinois. He remembered Bloomington, Illinois. Or was it Bloomington, Indiana? A university. Both towns had universities. A concert with The Trio. And then he knew it was *this* Bloomington, and the students were all seated on the floor around the stage. It was being recorded, a live performance. He could still see parts of it behind his eyes, hear and feel flashes of it. It was dark and hushed and the spotlight was terrible: bright and hot and over-dazzling. The music had gone perfectly, flawlessly, the way it was supposed to; and the audience was warm, responsive, silent with the pathos of their songs, clapping with the irony of others. And then he was backstage after the show in a stuffy dressing room and he was being told and urged and cajoled and bullied into going out to the front to talk to the audience. He resented that side of live concerts, refusing as much as possible, because it was not his music they wanted then, it was him; and it was not him they wanted, it was the image. And he didn't understand it, didn't want it. Yet he was told to sign autographs, meet audiences, sell records, sell the image, sell the next gig, sell his soul. And this time, he simply could not. He felt angry, and he felt betrayed. And then it all ran together and blurred for a moment, like the lights of the town outside the bus that were hurling themselves past the windows. That night of the long-ago concert, when the rest of the performers had gone out front without him, Kit knew he appeared temperamental, arrogant, and he didn't care. Immersed in his anger, content in his righteousness, he had walked out into the night and found a local bar with booths where he could sit unnoticed and hold on to a dark whiskey together with his dark mood. A young woman had slipped into the booth across from him and she had said simply, "Hi … my name's Zanna. Who are you?"

She had very long hair that was pale yellow and bright and it swung free and was backlit in the dim bar light creating halos reflecting off of it. She was too thin, but had an energy about her that was all strength and character and fearlessness. Her eyes were deep blue and heavy-lidded under the thickness of her lashes; they were eyes that listened deeply. She had freckles on top of her nose and across her cheek bones, with one particular one just under her right eye that Kit became particularly fond of. They talked through the night and found the best part of themselves in each other. When morning came, Kit had to leave with the others, but she promised to come find him in New York, and so she had; she arrived a few months later and had never gone back. She finished her journalism degree at NYU and had been picked up as a freelance writer ever since. Her work was sought after and worthy of it, and she was worth far more recognition than she received, Kit always felt, while he was never quite worthy of her himself. They found a small apartment together in Greenwich Village and she fell in love with Sam the dog and Kit the man. And then he had loved her too much and it had all gone wrong.

Kit slipped farther down in his bus seat and noticed that the woman next to him was sleeping lightly, her baby held so carefully, so protectively in her arms. Kit's heart twisted in guilt and pain, seeing Suzanna's face, her arms, empty. She wanted it all, and would find it all. And he knew it would not be with him. When they had talked the night before on the phone, Kit had told Suzanna not to come to Fort Wayne, for the funeral or for him, to stay in New York, to keep Sam safe with her, to keep the apartment in her name.

He knew he was saying goodbye to her as he was saying goodbye to his mother.

☾

It was 6:30 a.m. The sun was promising a morning soon. They had arrived in Fort Wayne, the last stop. Kit had helped the woman and her baby down the steep steps of the bus and then he retrieved his own baggage from its belly. He had turned to ask the woman for her name but she was gone. And so he began walking into the dawn, along streets that felt like they should be familiar but reacted like strangers to the sound of his footsteps, like people he didn't know avoiding his face as they hurried past him into their own mornings. He seemed to see scattered bits of his childhood in every storefront reflection and street sign name. But the old humming street lamps kept snapping off in front of him, as if their welcome was being withdrawn the closer he got to home.

It somehow surprised him when he suddenly came upon the old apartment house; he hadn't remembered it or the neighborhood looking so weary and small. And yet he didn't think it had been that long since his last visit. The sun was skimming the trees and they were deceiving in their beauty. The lushness of their turning colors absorbed the bleakness of the surroundings, transforming the debris in the streets beneath their own stunning litter.

The house cast a long shadow, matching his mindset and memories. He opened his wallet, and there was the old door key, its outline imprinted in the leather. He pulled the key loose, its brassy shine long rubbed away, leaving it bare. He walked up the few front porch steps and unlatched the street door into the small main-floor entry. He glanced with long habit at the open-faced mailboxes to the left of the interior stairs and saw there were some pieces stacked in the slot for his mother, so he grabbed them with his free fingers. And then he ascended the stairs to the second-floor apartment with great deliberation and an incoherent sense of hesitation and deliverance. Each step creaked with welcome and with shame, groaned with familiarity and with fear, and recalled every arrival and departure until the arrivals had stopped, until today.

At the top of the stairs, he looked over at Rene's door to the left, and knew she would be there. And he wondered with true affection what her hair would be like this time. Then he looked to the right, and his mother's door was blank and empty and he could feel her absence through its dark stained wood. Beneath the mat the key to the apartment door still waited. He wiped his feet and stood with shaking hands, unable to unlock the memories, to move past all the scratch marks on the lock face and the smoothness of the brass handle that gleamed from years of over-cleaning and being rubbed raw by his mother's hands, by his hands, and far too few others.

When at last he did find the need and courage to open the door, the smell of her enveloped him first, and then the silence. It was like the singular summary of his childhood – the delight and tragedy of it, the inglorious indifference of it, the sanctuary and the guilt and the bonds and the separation, all its love and loneliness and secrecy. He closed the door behind him, dropping his things around his feet where he stood. He walked into the bedroom and curled into the center of the bed fully clothed and fully naked. He pulled his legs up tight into his belly, his arms over his head, and he wept until he couldn't.

☽

The sun was high in the window, and he could feel it warm on his face, shining bright against his closed eyelids as he opened them slowly, reluctantly, remembering where he was and why he was there. He thought he heard soft knocking at the front door, listened with his head raised, then was sure of it. Without bothering to wipe his face or smooth down his hair, he went to the front of the apartment and caught Rene's soft, tortured face looking at him through the crack in the door she had opened with her own key.

"Hello, Kit," she said in quiet, unsure tones. "I hope you don't mind me letting myself in. I didn't know you were home until I saw your things here on the floor. How are you doing, Honey?"

He reached out and pulled the door wider for her. "Hi, Rene ... no that's fine. I'm glad you're here. I got in really early. What time is it?"

It was noon he saw just then on the kitchen wall clock in the next room as he started into the living room. "I must have fallen asleep for awhile," he nodded his head toward the bedroom.

"You remember this is the day of the funeral, right?" she reminded him. They had spoken briefly the morning he left Taos – which must have been the day before then, he calculated. And he had forgotten. They stood facing each other in the middle of the living room, neither one thinking to be seated.

"I really appreciate your taking care of everything, Rene – all the arrangements and everything – taking care of Mom. And for tracking me down. Thank you."

"Oh, of course, Honey. I was happy to do it. I mean, happy I could do it ... could help out. I loved you and your mother. We've been neighbors for such a long time. And family. She was very good to me over the years."

"You were very good to her, Rene. To both of us."

"The funeral is at 2:00 – at Saint Bartholomew's – and then Mrs. Blackstone and I thought you could invite people back here for coffee and sandwiches. Oh – not up here, Honey, not up here," she saw the look on Kit's face. "But down in Mrs. Blackstone's apartment. She has more room and she's already made the food. Just sandwiches – and her potato salad of course. I made a bundt cake. Just a small bunt cake. With cinnamon. It was your mother's favorite ..." Her voice got caught in her nose that she was pinching beneath a damp lace-edged handkerchief.

Kit put his arms around her and ducked in under her hair, which was stiff with hairspray and smelled of fresh coloring, a deep mahogany brown with streaks of yellow through it. But it felt good as they held each other close, familiar and comforting, and they clutched at each others' sadness and fears and impending loneliness for as many minutes as they could.

"Well," she patted him firmly on his back, "you go get ready, and I'll come back for you to walk to the church together."

Go get ready, he thought as she left him in the doorway. He had nothing with him in the way of nice clothes. Everything was still in New York, except what he had packed to ride the rails out to Taos. He had clean jeans (thanks to Roddy), and clean underwear (also thanks to Roddy). But he'd have to look in the bedroom closet to see if there was anything left there suitable in the way of a shirt and tie.

After a hot bath and an overdue shave, he tried to clean up his old scuffed boots. And then, putting on the best things he had with him – all on his lower half – he opened the bedroom closet door. His mother's scent breathed out at him again, ghost like, yet almost tangible, and it nearly took his knees out from under him. *Vol de Nuit, Vol de Nuit.* He could never forget it, could never be over the smell of her. And he stood there and just remembered. And then, slowly, he grabbed ahold of reality again and the reason why he was standing there. He straightened his body and carefully slid her hanging clothes to one side. It was a narrow but deep closet, and tall, with two double rows of hanging rods, one set behind the other. At the back and behind her heavier, winter dresses, he found two clean and pressed white shirts of his – from how long ago, he didn't know, but they seemed to be waiting there for him, stiff and shaped by the wire hangers; and next to them was an old sport jacket: a rough herringbone tweed, with a cut and lapels that were only slightly out of date. He remembered leaving it there one Thanksgiving, but it seemed a very long time ago, too. There were no ties that he could see. But he thought this might be okay; and so when he had them on, he brushed his teeth and combed his hair and he went to find Rene. But first, he ran down to the basement; just as he had done for so many years whenever he was in need of understanding, he went to find Bruno.

He realized he was knocking on Bruno's door louder and more insistently than he had intended. And when the aging man opened the door to him, Kit could not find any words other than, "My mom died, Bruno, she died."

"I know of it, Christopher. I know of it. You will be coming in now," Bruno said in his slow, thoughtful, broken voice.

"I need to go to the funeral now. Will you come?" Kit looked at Bruno and took in his movements that spoke of hard pain and long fatigue. But he saw, too, that he was dressed in a suit, bagged and shiny with age, and he had on a clean blue work shirt and an old tie.

"Yes, Christopher, I will be coming too. Yes."

"I need to get Rene, but will you walk with us to the church?"

"I am walking too slow now, too much slow. You go, you go. I will be there when these old legs are bringing me." He started to wave Kit away.

"Thank you, Bruno. Thank you. You look very nice. I've never seen you wearing a suit and tie before. You look nice."

"Christopher – you are having no tie at your neck?" Bruno suddenly squinted at him.

"I didn't pack one, I'm afraid."

"A boy must be wearing a tie for his mama," Bruno said with assurance, as he reached up and unfastened his own tie and put it around Kit's neck, tucking it under his collar. "It is good."

The tie was terribly old and too short and clashed woefully with Kit's sport coat, but Kit smiled and nodded at Bruno as he pressed it against his heart, and then he tied it carefully, and tucked it into his jacket and he went to collect Rene.

Saint Bartholomew's Episcopalian Church was just two blocks from the house. It had been his mother's church for as long as Kit could remember. And for most of his childhood he had been taken to Sunday school there, listened to stories and put his pennies in the collection basket. And then he'd been placed firmly next to his mother on a hard pew for long services. He'd gone through the motions of communion and sung in the choir. He'd been especially called upon to sing in the choir and he'd enjoyed that part of it. He'd also memorized his way through confirmation classes, and taken his turn at being an alter boy; he smiled as he remembered his duties as an acolyte, finding the responsibilities confusing, but delighting in making people choke on the over abundance of incense he swung in their direction, until he thought the priest probably caught on to him and graduated the next boy up to the role. He'd always felt uncomfortable with the formality of it all, the ritualistic practices; he couldn't stop seeing it as something out of the movies just before the sacrifice of the virgins or the revelation of the man behind the curtain.

    Except for the random Christmas visits home, he hadn't been back to St. Bart's since he'd moved to New York. And he thought about how he'd felt an undeniably closer connection to the spirituality he'd found in Taos in the past few weeks than he ever had at the church. But it felt right to be there on this day, for this purpose. And so he allowed himself to be led and directed through all the funereal ceremonies, his memory taking over for active thought as he knelt on the red-cushioned fold-down platform in front of the pew, and took the tasteless wafer on his tongue and sipped from the cup, and listened to the priest's words of attempted comfort. He did not sing the hymns, but he thought instead of Chaplain Locke in Huntsville, and he remembered the sound and smell of the old Indian spirit in the damp hallway, and he relived the visions of the young boy and the old woman in white in Taos. And then he brought himself into the present as they threaded their way out to the gravesite behind the sanctuary.

There were not many in attendance; his mother's circle of friends was notably small. A few coworkers left over from the bank where she worked, several members from the church. Kit sat alone, and Rene sat directly behind him, her bracelets jangling as a reminder that she was nearby if needed. Bruno sat alone, too, at the very back. But there was no one there just for him, just for his comfort, for his own grief. He had let his friends drift away from that town, as he had drifted away from everything else. But when he saw Jacob's mother and father beside the grave, he embraced them for it and let himself fold into Jacob's mother's arms with unspeakable gratitude.

When the others had departed from the open churchyard grave, Kit remained for a long while, sitting next to his mother; Bruno moved forward and sat with him, silent, knowing. Even the priest eventually grew tired and went back into the church. Rene had already preceded everyone back to the apartment house to receive the guests.

Kit put his hand into his side coat pocket and pulled out the precious white corn charm, the Mah-pah-róo that Anita had made for him. Carefully, gently, he untied the cornhusks and unrolled the burlap that wrapped it. He touched the softness of the white feathers with the tips of his fingers, and the edges of the coral and the turquoise and the silver that hung from its sides, and he admired its beauty.

"And have you ever wondered why the moon has one eye?" Kit quoted softly. Bruno heard but did not interrupt. "She was blinded for her child and to her child and about her child and because of her child … and so she could not see the darkness, her darkness, his darkness," he chanted to himself, about himself.

Kit stood up and reached out to the top of the casket, and he placed the native symbol on top of it, tucking it securely under the edge of the wreath that was already wilting there, so that it would enter the grave and eternity with her. And he said quite softly: "Goodbye, Mother."

And then without looking at Bruno, he asked him: "What if I cannot forgive her? Or me? Where do I find the forgiveness, if it's not in my heart?"

Bruno did not look up, but he waited a moment and then he said quietly, subtly: "You give mercy, Christopher." He paused again, and Kit listened to the old man's breathing, deep in his throat. Then Bruno continued, "Forgiveness is not needed always. But 'Blessed are the merciful,' yes? And so, you give the mercy. To her – and to you. And that is good enough. Yes. Mercy is good. It is enough." Kit looked at Bruno from the corner of his eye, and he listened to him breathe, and he nodded.

Eventually, Kit and Bruno walked home, slowly, painfully. They talked about mercy and butterflies.

By the time they reached the house, Bruno said he would not stop in at Mrs. Blackstone's but would go on down to his rooms, and Kit said he'd fix a plate for him and bring it down later. Kit removed and returned Bruno's tie to him with great care and appreciation.

Kit let himself into Mrs. Blackstone's apartment as she was just clearing away most of the used plates and cups. The mourners had gone, with the exception of Rene and another woman that Kit did not seem to recognize. Rene put her arm around him at the door and brought him into the room to meet the stranger.

"Honey, this is Mrs. Kaye Kline. She was your mother's lawyer. She did up her will and all, and she's been waiting to talk to you." Rene then excused herself with a foil-covered plate already made up for Bruno and she said she'd be right back.

Mrs. Kline led Kit over to the sofa before saying quietly, "It is good to meet you, Kit. I was hoping we could talk soon. Would it be possible for you to come to my office tomorrow, in the morning? If you are up to it. We need to address some of your mother's legal issues." She hesitated over the last words, and then she handed him one of her business cards. It was embossed on thick cream-colored paper and used pitch black ink and showed that she was in practice for herself. He thought she was probably in her mid to late fifties and she spoke with a strong accent, perhaps German, perhaps Eastern European; it reminded him of Bruno, yet different somehow. Her English was far superior to the handyman's, but he thought perhaps she had been in this country longer, had more practice. Her hair was dark and heavy, and there was a wide streak of pure white in it, running from her right temple up into the mass of curls she had pulled behind her ear and secured with a carved tortoise-shell comb; it aligned perfectly with the streak of white scar that clipped the end of her right eyebrow and ran down her jaw and behind the scarf around her neck. It was as if she were showcasing it.

"Yes, of course," Kit responded. At first he felt slightly offended, as if this was somehow greedy and unnecessary. But the woman herself intrigued him, and she seemed authentic and kind and genuinely interested in talking to him, so there was nothing else for him to do but agree. He had not known that his mother had an attorney. Or even a will. Or a need for either one.

When the lawyer had gone, Mrs. Blackstone insisted that he stay and have something to eat. Rene was back and stayed too. They talked about the old days when Kit was "the boy" growing up among them, and they remembered things and they remembered his mother. And in their kindness, they did not ask about Suzanna, but they did ask about where he had been and what he had been doing. And so he diverted them by telling them all about Wade.

Mrs. Blackstone was busying herself with turning on lamps and whisking crumbs from tables. The sun had already set and they were waiting to take their leave of one another until they felt they were no longer needed. Kit looked fondly around him before he stood to go upstairs. He thought that even the hanging plants were the same, along with everything else in that room that was recorded in his memory: the old black-and-white television on a wheeled cart; the sofa that scratched young bare legs and smelled of stale tobacco and spaghetti sauce; the low blond-wood coffee table that held a TV Guide and plastic coasters and one leggy plant on its top, with stacks of National Geographics on a lower shelf; the single arm chair that faced both the sofa and the television at an angle and had wooden arms and an upholstered seat and a loose cushion back that didn't quite match, with a footstool in front of it that carried the inexplicable scratchings of a cat, although Kit could never remember a cat ever living in that apartment and he had never been allowed to ask about it. He still couldn't.

They wished each other a goodnight and shared their sadness once again, and Kit walked Rene upstairs and then let himself into his mother's apartment. He thought about calling Suzanna, and he thought about going down to see Bruno again, but he did neither; instead, he opened the gift from Roddy that she'd packed in his food sack. It was wrapped in newspaper and smelled a bit of bread and cheese.

Kit knew it was fragile, based on the way Roddy had gently touched the sides of the sack when she gave it to him, and because of the layers of protective paper she had wound around it, so he unrolled it carefully against his legs as he sat on the sofa. The last bit of paper around it was the letter that Roddy had written for him in explanation. He smiled at seeing her familiar, artistic, perfect handwriting; but he was in awe of the gift as it revealed itself. He admired it for several minutes before he turned his attention to the letter:

Dear Kit:
    This is a treasure I have had with me for ages – but I want you to have it now. The glass sphere was hand

blown by an artist friend of mine. And the single feather contained within it is one that I found not long after I moved to Taos.

You may remember that I was on my own for the first time when I came here, to find my art, my personal expression. I was out exploring around the old Taos Pueblo very early one morning – just at sunrise, just at that liminal time when it is not yet day but not still night.

I remember I was walking with one of the first dogs I took in, and we were at the edge of that branch of the Rio Grande that runs past the Pueblo. Out of nowhere swept this amazing, almost magical bird. It was a great blue heron, and it had an unimaginable span of blue-black wings, with a perfectly silent flight, perfect in its grace. It took my breath away as I watched it. Even the dog stood absolutely still and just watched with me. It had come to rest on a tree limb that reached out across the river's edge, and it watched us in return – in a slow-rising mist.

After awhile, the dog and I began to walk on, and the bird spread its wings again, and flew across our path once more, still silent and mysterious and wonderfully close. And then it sort of glided around the bend in the river, and it was gone. But at my feet, there was a single, perfect feather – the feather that is now enclosed in this glass sphere.

I talked to Anita and some of the other Indians about the encounter, and they told me about all the wonderful qualities of the heron as a spirit animal in their culture – things like patience, solitude, independence, and just being in the present – things I was searching for, that I was needing in my life right then. And so I had the feather protected in glass.

And now I want you to have it. But I think, for you, it is also significant that the heron is a creature that is comfortable in all three elements – earth, water, and air – able to live in balance with them all. So it serves well as a spirit guide for moving through times of change in our lives – the times of transition.

There is one final bit about it that I think is important: If you hold this feather against a background of light, it will look dark to you; but if you hold it against the dark, it will appear light. I will leave it to you to make of that what you will – and to let it speak to your own heart.

Be well and happy, my dear friend,
Roddy.

Kit held the feather in glass up to the light and watched it floating in its space. It was surprisingly long – at least eight or nine inches. And it was almost plume-like with individual fingers of it reaching out and away from its center spine, from top to bottom, with a long peak at the very top and tuffs of fluff covering the bottom of the shaft. It was both delicate and sure, something of the air and of the earth. And he watched it change from dark to light to dark to light again as he moved it around the room and against various backgrounds and perspectives; and he wondered if his own darkness and light might be much like the feather – according to perspective, and how he chose to hold it.

That night Kit slept not in the bed, but on the living room couch, under a blanket he found at the back of the hall closet. And that night he dreamed he was walking alone across dew-soaked grasses near water, and his feet made no sound as he moved closer and closer to the creature hidden in the shadows there. Suddenly, it spread its wings and he saw it was a great blue heron. It covered him with its warm, downy expanse, and he could hear its heartbeat even as he slept.

The heartbeats were there again, and again they were reaching out to him through the haze of that sleep that overtakes exhaustion. He turned his ear and mind to them more closely, and then he heard them for what they were – not heartbeats, but the rhythmic sound of tires, tires beating themselves along dark gray highways, bus tires thudding him on his way to another Texas prison. And this time, he would not be leaving it for at least five years, perhaps longer.

Kit had known he was guilty, and he was found guilty, and he was to be punished accordingly. The punishment would also take into consideration the fact that he had mysteriously disappeared for several months, out of contact with his probation officer, with no explanation, no permission. Kit had pleaded no contest. And Steve had asked the prison board for and gotten him into a minimum-security facility.

The sentence was beginning that afternoon, at the end of the bus ride, at the end of the gray highway, at the end of the day. Kit made the trip in silence and thought. He wondered if he would have a window in his cell. And he wondered if he would be able to see the moon.

The day he received the phone call telling him he had to report to the Texas law authorities was the day after his mother's funeral. It was the same day he'd learned he had inherited just over a million dollars.

🌙

He had lost his mother. He had gained great wealth. He was going to prison.

The vast disparity – yet strange connectedness – between these sudden realities for Kit left his sense of self mocked by a mix of chaos and closure. The two Kits had somehow reached their respective destinies on the same afternoon of October 3, 1972. Earth to earth, dust to dust, ashes to ashes. And he had become at peace with himself, in sync with himself, and as near to self-healing as he was to self-destruction. A unique place of being for him.

He would unfold and reread and refold Roddy's letter many times, and he would cling to her prophetic gift and its truth: the feather in a bottle, the feather of the great blue heron, the great blue heron that was the spirit guide through change and transition, liminal times and places of uncertainty. The great blue heron that was at home in all of the elements of earth, water, air – and found balance between them. And he felt he was not much more than a particle of that earth, a reflection of water, a breath of air. Balanced on the head of a pin.

He would unfold and return to the memory of that day in Kay Kline's office many times as well. There was a blitz of sun off the golden dome of the Court House across the street from her office building, the clock was chiming the hour, the old door pulled against gusts of autumn wind; and there was a fresh-cut smell of the flower shop on the ground floor – heady, wild, green, wet. Mrs. Kline's law office was on the second floor of the old building, with windows in the reception area overlooking the courthouse itself. Her clerk seemed painfully inhibited as he ushered Kit into the lawyer's private office. It was all dark woods and glinting windows, oriental rugs and huge vases of fresh cut flowers, and layers of leather-bound books. There was a very European sense of place about it. Her desk was crescent shaped, wrapping around a high-backed leather chair. In front of the desk were two more chairs – cracked leather, rolled arms, rather like WWI ace flier jackets without the long white silk scarves and goggles. The clerk served them both dark coffee and frosted buns.

Mrs. Kline had opened a thick accordion-fold file folder that was on the top of her desk, and she pulled out what looked like a small black address book. Putting the little book down on the desk top, she slid it over to him with her index finger. "This is your mother's Swiss bank account. Now it is yours."

And that's how he found out. His first and only awareness of its existence. And all he could hear after that was his mother's voice, her words, her preconceptions.

> Swiss bank accounts are for the rich and for criminals. Nothing good or right was ever kept in a Swiss bank account. It's bad luck to have one ... terribly wrong ...

But Mrs. Kline went on with the story: "You should know that I was born in Warsaw, Poland. And when I was 19 years old, the Nazis came and invaded my home, tortured and killed my parents, my sisters ... Well, I will assume you know your history. But unless you lived during it ... lived through it ..." She had raised her hand and had run her fingers along the scar on her face and then smoothed the scarf around her neck. "Friends were able to get me out – and I survived." And Kit watched her fingers, and his mind followed them along the white healing path that defined her face and being, along with his own connected and disconnected memories, his own healing path.

> Scars ... scars and wounds and
> escapes ... fear and running ...
> running and trains ...
> trains and tramps ... Bruno and Wade
> ... survival ...

"I am telling you all this because you should know why your mother came to me." Mrs. Kline had spoken about herself detached and monotoned, as if talking about someone else's life, and Kit understood with his own insight.

> Two women ... two boys ... divide and
> conquer ... split apart and live apart
> ... escape and survive ...

"When your mother inherited this Swiss account, she knew that many people in Europe had hidden their money and jewels and gold in such a way during the war. And some of this money and these valuables were gained in not good ways. Some of it was even stolen from Jews as they were put into camps or killed – although some of it was put there for legitimate safekeeping to help them protect their assets." She nodded as she spoke these last words, as if to reinforce an acknowledgement of that truth. "But regardless, since the war, there have been many difficulties in making sure it is returned to the rightful owners.

I am a Jew and I am a lawyer, and I am involved with these efforts." But Kit's mind could focus only on the lies – his mother's lies.

> She would not ... she would not
> have had such an account ...
> she would not ... unless she lied to me
> ... she lied and ... she lied ...

And then Mrs. Kline had asked him what he knew about his mother's French ancestry, and he told her what he could call to mind: Of the one day when he was very young, a little boy standing behind his mother's dressing table, and she was telling him: "*Vol de Nuit* ... it's called *Vol de Nuit*" ... she was dabbing perfume on her wrists and the soft bends of her elbows, behind her ears, and down the front of her throat. "It's French, and it means Night Flight – isn't that a romantic name, Kit – *Vol de Nuit* ... Night Flight. It was your grandmother's scent ... and her mother's. Her family owned the company where it was made. They were very important people in their town in France, Kit. Remember that – your mother comes from a very important French family." And then he was at an air show with Rene and her sausage-curled hair and her long hat – and Rene was telling him about his grandfather building planes for the Morane-Saulnier company. But it was not his grandfather, it was his *great* grandfather. And his mother had told him too, once, when he was too young, about his great grandfather being a very important pilot and an inventor. And she told Kit that he must always remember – "Your mother comes from a very important French family."

But he had not remembered. And he had not thought of the two stories as belonging together. And he had not thought of any of it as even real.

And so Mrs. Kline made it real: "Your family's wealth came from two sources – perfumes, your great grandmother's heritage; and aircraft, your great grandfather's legacy. I know the airplane company where your great grandfather worked came under German control and operation during the second world war, and that, I suspect, is why your mother's fears and reluctance about the money began to take such a hold on her – because of the assets added to it during that tragic time.

"Your great grandparents had only one child – your grandmother. And your mother was her only child. So the bank account has been handed down in a straight maternal line since its inception. Your mother didn't inherit this account – or was not notified of it anyway – until after the war, after her parents and grandparents were all gone, and the world was trying desperately to forget, and yet all the time more and more terribly atrocities were being uncovered. She had no one to advise her. Your father was not someone … no. And in her mind – in the minds of many during that time – anything to do with a Swiss bank account was highly suspect, tainted, immoral. I met your mother when I spoke at her church. And she saw me as someone who could be trusted to look into the legitimacy of her family's account without prejudice – that I could take this out of her hands and I would do what was right. She had not so much as even written a letter to the bank or responded to their correspondence. She was just so terrified that it was ill-gotten and would somehow bring terrible things down on her head – perhaps onto your head – if she accepted it, or even acknowledged that it was in her family. But she trusted me to do the right thing. It's all legitimate, Kit. It's all real. It belongs to you."

And then Kit had signed pages and pages of documents and initialed them in dozens and dozens of places and the clerk made copies for him and put them into an envelope to take with him tucked under his arm. And Mrs. Kline gave him an envelope with cash in it, and a credit card and a checking account and she tried to talk to him about what his options were, and the clerk insisted on giving him fresh coffee and just one more bun. Until Kit made them just stop. And he left the papers on one of the office chairs and said he would call for them later. And he walked out of the building and into the beautiful autumn air where he could finally fully breathe.

Eventually, he came to a local tobacconist shop and he bought some very expensive cigars with the very old money he had found in the envelope, and then he found a small park with weathered benches and he sat alone and smoked one of the very expensive cigars. And he let his betrayal and confusion and clarity and truth all exhale from him, curl above his head, lift away with the wind, along with the cigar smoke.

> Do the right thing ... hurt the right people ... betray the right people ... leave the right people ... make the right things feel wrong, the right people feel wrong. So many secrets, so much money, so much, too much.

And now it's too late. She took
too much from me ... and then she gave
too much to me ... it's too much, too
late. Riding buses late at night ...
long cold walks to school ... shoes
too tight, worn thin ... struggling
for scholarships ... struggling for
space in one bed ... trying to breathe,
hearing her breathe ... rolling too
close ... rolling pennies
... stealing cars ... siphoning gas ...
selling drugs ... waiting for bail ...
sacrificing Suzanna. Suzanna sold her
pearls ... I sold my soul ... I sold my
soul to please her. She made me
keep her sordid secrets ... but she was
the greatest secret keeper ...
she kept secrets from me.
I was too young ... just a little boy
who wanted to please ... I tried so
hard to be the good boy. And now she
has given me this secret and this money
and they are too much, too late ...
too much, too late.
Let there be mercy ... can there be
mercy? ... should there be mercy? ...
be merciful to the blind ... she was
half blind for me ... she was half
blind about me ... she was half blind
from fear. She loved me too much.
And may God and Bruno and I have mercy
on her soul.

Mrs. Kline sat down next to Kit on the park bench and handed him a paper cup still steaming with coffee.

"It's not as good as my clerk makes, but it'll do," she said without looking at him.

Kit took the cup in silence. He had believed he wanted to be alone with it all, but he realized he welcomed her presence. Perhaps he had hoped for it.

"Tell me about it," she said in a matter-of-fact voice. It wasn't a request. It was permission. And then she reached into her oversized, overpriced handbag and lifted out a silver flask. It smelled of expensive brandy as she liberally laced both their coffees with its contents.

Kit pulled a deep drink of the liquid, and then pulled the hot cigar smoke deep into his lungs. He held it there for a few long seconds, and then slowly let it loose in jagged puffs and scraps. But still the words did not form.

"For me," she got him started, "it sometimes comes through like those old-fashioned camera flash bulbs that would sort of burst open the darkness, and then leave behind orbs of blindness – and pain. But then the picture becomes clear. And eventually I can look at it. And then I can put it away." She gazed up at the trees overhead and pulled her coat tighter around her.

"I hear sounds, sometimes," he said. "Or feel things against my skin."

"Give me some," she said, still not looking at him.

And he found himself telling her: "I'm in the bathroom. I'm in the tub with just a small amount of water around me. The water's cold. I think I must be very young. I hear my parents out in the living room – loud voices, yelling, fighting. But I can't understand the words.

I don't know the words. But I hear my name, and I know the fight is about me. And then I hear my dad leaving the house – slamming the door. My mother's crying – crying with her hard voice. And I see her standing in the bathroom doorway looking at me and crying. And she grabs me up out of the bath. I'm shivering. And she is holding me so tight, too tight. It hurts. She has buttons on her dress – all down the front of her dress - and they scrape against my naked skin. They hurt. And I try to put my hand between us or pull back, but she just tightens her hold on me. I want her to stop. But she's too strong. I'm not strong enough. And then she's saying something soft, using her soft voice, singing and sobbing, and telling me she loves me, but it keeps hurting me. I thought if my dad were there he would help me. But my dad's not there. He doesn't come to help me."

Kit leaned forward on the bench, rested his arms across his legs and held the cigar in one hand, the coffee in the other. And he felt the pain – vague, yet still real – across his back. "I was late coming home from school once – maybe in the third grade – we'd just moved into the new apartment and I'd gotten lost walking home. It was nearly dark. Mother was waiting for me on the sidewalk. I could tell she was terrified. I kept trying to tell her I was sorry. She pulled me up the stairs by one arm. And I kept stumbling. And then she held me across the arm of a chair – held me down with her knee – and pulled down my pants. She was beating me with a wooden spoon and crying; hitting me harder and harder and all the time she was crying. And then, suddenly, it stopped, but she kept crying and started kissing my back and buttocks where she had beaten me and telling me she loved me. And I could feel her tears against my raw skin. They stung. They stung the brokenness. And she kept telling me how much we loved each other. And that she was my mother and so I had to forgive her. I just wanted to say I was sorry."

Mrs. Kline still had not spoken. But she had opened her handbag again and rummaged through it until she found a pack of cigarettes. She pulled one free and held it to her lips. It was long and black and the pack looked foreign to Kit as he watched her light it with a small gold lighter that glinted in the sun. She blew the smoke into the air.

"My god, those stink," Kit couldn't help commenting.

"They're Russian. They're disgusting. But I got addicted years ago." She studied the toe of her shoe for awhile as she and Kit sat is silence. "Sometimes, we get addicted to rotten things," she said thoughtfully.

And Kit knew she was talking about him, encouraging him to continue telling her his secrets without shame.

And so he told her about how his mother used to climb naked into the tub with him when she was giving him a bath. And she'd wash his hair and tell him stories and rub him gently all over with the soap. And he remembered when it started to make his stomach feel bad and his head feel dizzy and he tried to get out, but she pulled him back and he learned to somehow separate his mind from his body. To shut his eyes. To shut his mind. To turn off his body. And then he told her how he used to become two boys. And one of them lived behind the refrigerator in the alcove. And only one of them had to take the baths … had to sleep in her bed … had to smell her perfume.

And then he told her about sleeping over at Jacob's and his other friends' houses as much as he could. He saw how their mothers' didn't dress them or touch them all the time. And he felt different around them. And he knew, when he was as tall as his mother, and the spanking had stopped, that he should make her stop caressing him. Stop bathing him. Stop brushing his hair. Stop making him sleep in her bed. If only she would just buy him his own bed.
    After more remembrances, more pain, more silences, Mrs. Kline asked: "What happened when you started dating girls? Did you date girls?"
    "Oh, yes. And she became even more possessive – but very sly about it, and more generous at the same time. She bought me things. Gave me gifts that we couldn't afford. And I took them."
    "Did you ever tell anyone any of this?"
    "I wanted to talk to my dad, but by then he was always drunk – always. And I thought about confiding in Rene – but it would have just embarrassed her, I think – and she would have told my mom. I knew Bruno would listen. But no one would have listened to Bruno."
    "Why not a priest or a teacher?"
    "It wasn't polite."
    "Why didn't you just say 'no' to your mother?"
    "I wish I knew." Kit looked down at his hands as they rested in his lap and he felt warm tears on them, but didn't recognized them as his own. He watched the cigar burn cold, with ash clinging crookedly to its end. His breath came just as crookedly as he caught sight of the rising moon: "I was just a little boy. And she was my mother. And we loved each other."

Kit stood slowly, stiffly, and held out his hand to Mrs. Kline. "I wonder if my mother never acknowledged the truth about the Swiss bank account – or her family wealth that she had to know about – because she just never acknowledged truth."

It was almost dark by the time he got back to his mother's apartment. The phone was ringing. It was his New York lawyer, Joel Menken, telling him he was wanted in Texas.

He had lost his mother. He had gained great wealth. He was going to prison. But he had told someone the truth. He had told himself the truth.

After the first few days and weeks of his life imprisoned, Kit settled into a not unpleasant routine. He was confined with only a few hundred other men in this minimum security facility. He had his own cell with his own toilet accommodation behind a semi-private wall, although showers were taken at appointed times in appointed places. He had a desk and chair, a reasonably comfortable bed, institutional food that was at least hot and on time and filling. He was allowed to be in the outside air and sun and to exercise with only a few restrictions. And he had a window – where the moon still eluded and refused him most nights.

Conversation with the other prisoners and guards was at least cordial, relatively intelligent, but highly depressing. And so he chose to be alone for the most part, and he spent hours in the library or reading in his cell, writing long letters to no one but himself. He kept the writings in a thick brown leather journal that Roddy had sent him; handmade, filled with blank pages of heavy paper, although the pen had to be allotted to him from the prison supply in lieu of his favorite fountain pen.

Then, one day, he began writing the letters to Suzanna, and he wondered why he never mailed them. In the letters he watched the black ink fill the paper, page after page. He wrote about why the more he loved her, the less he was able to physically express that love to her. The closer he felt to her, the farther away he pulled. And he knew he was complicit in the ruin of their life together, their possibilities – all because he had never said "no" to his mother.

But then he thought about his mother. And how much they loved each other. And he closed the journal and put the cap on the pen and went to the window to watch for the moon.

And so, day-by-day, one much like any other, seven hundred and thirty-one of them passed. In 1973, the Texas laws about marijuana changed, and Steve Silva had not forgotten him. Two years and one day after beginning his punishment, Kit was forgiven.

Kit had just finished the last song for the night – the song he performed to close most of his sets now. It was slow, soft, not quite a love song. A reflection. A portrait of a woman who had once loved him – completely, gently, blindly, too much. But it seemed authentic, ironic and sad, full of remembrance and gratitude and sorrow. It was, perhaps, like a beautiful and broken piece of himself that would trail along after him for the rest of his life.

And so it became a nightly anthem for him. Always at closing. Always at the end. Always just before he told the staff "good night" – and thanked them for a good night.

And this night he told them that they should all go home then, that he'd lock up, and that they could clean up in the morning. "Beat the storm," he said, as the wind rushed at them, the rain needle sharp against the windows. A real Fort Wayne, northern Indiana, autumn storm. Bitter and blustery, but rarely any thunder or lightning. Fearsome, yet somehow fear-less.

Kit continued to run his fingers along the keyboard. And the old brewery building soaked up the notes as if they were still the beads of damp that used to glisten down its copper fermentation tanks. Kit had been captivated by the century-old building when he first saw it, empty, ghosted even then with cobwebs and echos of industry. He was just in his teens. But he had felt the history of the place, was charmed by its architecture, its brick and stone, its wood floors and ceiling beams, its glass window panes that bent the light and reshaped the images on the other side. He doted on its character, the brass light fixtures and door knobs and copper downspouts. He saw before and beyond all the broken glass and sagging roofline. And he promised himself that he would one day own this building – perhaps live in it, perhaps open a club there, where he would serve excellent food and the best beers and wines, and where he would sing for his customers, where he would sing for his mother.

And then he forgot. Almost a quarter of a century passed before he saw his building again. Remarkably, no one else had seen its value, before its value began to decline steadily into the surrounding rubble and weeds. But after Kit's release from prison in Texas, he had returned to Fort Wayne, because that was where he had left himself, and he had found the building again as well. It had stood there waiting before him one evening at dusk as he walked the old streets of the original edges of town. And he had called Mrs. Kaye Kline, his financial advisor and keeper of secrets, and he had told her to buy it for him. She had shared and understood his vision, his need for the project, and she played a great part in its restoration and renewal.

It took on its reclaimed life and purpose as: Kit's Place. And Kit did live in an apartment created on its top floors. And it did become well known for its excellent food and the best beers and wines. But mostly it became a favorite for its atmosphere and experiential sense of place, built around its nightly entertainment – of new talent given a chance, and of old musicians passing through, and of Kit himself performing those songs that had brought him his original fame along with those songs that he and Wade had written in Taos.

The restoration of the broken building became the reflection of the man. It was a rebuilding from the shattered bits and pieces left behind when everything else had gone away, had left his life.

While he was in prison, Mrs. Blackstone had finally grown weary and given up waiting for her husband to return, and so she had sold the old apartment house and moved to a condominium in Arizona. She made the people who bought the property promise to keep Bruno on as handyman with as light a workload as possible, and to let him continue living in his apartment, which they promised to do and signed papers saying they would do, but then they simply forgot about him – until they found him, alone, sick, and dying. Rene had already moved away with a new husband. It surprised everyone, most of all Rene herself. But his name was Harry and he was also a beautician, and they set up a small shop of their own in the front room of a house he owned in Defiance, Ohio, and they were rather content and successful.

Before Kit bought and converted the old brewery, he had, for awhile, considered returning to Taos. And then he had discovered that it held for him so much mystique and memory, such saving grace and healing power, and a haunting sense of spirituality that he couldn't let himself lose that – feared it would fade away if he returned to its reality. And then Roddy and Wade moved to Santa Fe – for Roddy's art, and for the wild mustangs that Wade had been wanting to photograph before he found Roddy in Taos instead.

New York would forever remain in the past for Kit. The last time he had spoken to Suzanna was when he had sent her all of the bond money, after his sentencing. And then she had written to him, telling him that she was moving out of their Greenwich Village apartment – too much of him and of them together was still there, she said.

And she told him that Sam was gone, had died in his sleep, and she had known it was coming so she had held him in her lap in the old rocking chair until she felt his last breath.

☾

The storm wailed around the old converted brewery building. It pressed its face against the windows in long wet sighs and shuddering outbursts. And periodically, the wind would lunge and stamp its wet boots, carrying the rain high on its slick back. And it began to play tricks with the lights, and awaken ghosts and shake them loose from their resting places.

"Good night, Boss," Kit heard the familiar voices of his staff cut through the sounds of the wind and rain.

And he answered back: "Be safe out there."

"See you tomorrow, Kit," the last voice leaving called out to him.

"Yes."

And then, with a final whip and rush of wind trying to get through the door as it latched itself tightly between himself and the wildness outside, he saw her shadow coming toward him. And she was shaking the rain from her coat and her hair. And she walked into his light, and she sat down next to him, and she said: "Hi ... my name's Zanna ... who are you?"

And so he found himself telling her about it all – from Texas to Taos, to the truth and back again. And he sang for her, and he held her there. Until the storm rode itself out on the wind. The morning came. And she faded away with the moon.